W9-DHF-204

FIC
TEM

FIRST EDITION
Second Printing

Copyright © 1976 by R. L. Templeton

Published in The United States Of America
By Eakin Publications, Inc.
P.O. Box 23066, Austin, Texas 78735

Library of Congress Catalogue Card No. 76-5298
ISBN 0-89015-119-9

DEDICATION

This book is respectfully dedicated to the 182 men who died on March 6, 1836, defending the Alamo. A special dedication is bestowed on the 8 Mexican-Texans who lost their lives. I name them first:

(1) Gregorio Esparaza—who had a brother fighting outside the walls with Santa Anna's Army.
(2) Juan Abamillo, from San Antonio
(3) Carlos Espallier, San Antonio
(4) Antonio Fuentes, San Antonio
(5) Andres Nava, San Antonio
(6) Juan Badillo, San Antonio
(7) J. Losoya
(8) R. Rodriguez
The other 173 men who died for the Independence of Texas are:
(1) R (poe) Allen
(2) Miles DeForest Andros, San Patricio, Texas
(3) Micajah Autry, North Carolina or Tennessee
(4) Peter James Bailey, Arkansas & Tennessee
(5) Isaac Baker, Gonzales, Texas
(6) William Charles M. Baker, Missouri
(7) John J. Ballentine, Alabama
(8) John J. Baugh (Major) Virginia
(9) Joseph Bayliss, Tennessee
(10) John Blair
(11) Samuel P. Blair, Tennessee
(12) William Blazeby, England, via New York
(13) James Butler Bonham (Colonel), South Carolina & Alabama
(14) Dan Bourne, Eng.
(15) Jim Bowie, Arkansas
(16) George Brown, England
(17) James Brown, Pennsylvania
(18) Robert Brown
(19) James Buchannan, Alabama
(20) Samuel E. Burnell, Louisiana & Ireland
(21) George Butler, Missouri
(22) John Cane, Pennsylvania
(23) William R. Carey, Maryland
(24) Charles Henry Clark. Missouri
(25) M.B. Clark, Nacogdoches, Texas
(26) Daniel William Cloud, Kentucky & Arkansas
(27) Robert E. Cochran, New Jersey
(28) George Washington Cottle, Missouri
(29) Henry Courtman, Germany
(30) Lemuel Crawford, South Carolina

(31) David Crockett, Tennessee
(32) Robert Crossman, Louisiana, Massachusetts
(33) David P. Cummings, Pennsylvania
(34) Robert Cunningham, New York
(35) Jacob C. Durst, Kentucky
(36) Freeham H.K. Day, Gonzales, Texas
(37) Jerry C. Day, Missouri
(38) Squire Daymon, Tennessee
(39) William Dearduff, Tennessee
(40) Stephen Denison, Ireland, via Kentucky
(41) Charles Despallier, Louisiana
(42) Almeron Dickinson, (Lieutenant/Captain) Tennessee, Penn.
(43) John H. Dillard, Tennessee
(44) James H. Dimpkins, England
(45) Louis Duel, New York
(46) Andrew Duvalt, Ireland
(47) Robert Evans (Major) (Master of Ordinance), Ireland, New York
(48) Samuel B. Evans, Kentucky
(49) James L. Ewing, Tennessee
(50) William Fishbaugh, Gonzales, Texas
(51) John Flanders, Massachusetts
(52) Dolphin Ward Floyd, North Carolina
(53) John Hubbard Forsyth, New York
(54) Galba Fuqua, Gonzales, Texas
(55) William H. Furtleroy, Kentucky
(56) William Garnett, Virginia
(57) James Girrard Garrett, Tennessee
(58) James W. Garrand, Louisiana
(59) John E. Garvin, Gonzales, Texas
(60) John E. Gaston, Kentucky
(61) James George, Gonzales, Texas
(62) John Camp Goodrich, Tennessee
(63) Albert Calvin Grimes, Georgia
(64) James G. Gwynne, England
(65) James Hannum, Refugio, Texas
(66) John Harris, Kentucky
(67) Andrew Jackson Harrison
(68) William B. Harrison, Ohio
(69) Joseph M. Hawkins, Ireland, via Louisiana
(70) John M. Hays, Tennessee
(71) Charles M. Heiskell, Tennessee
(72) Thomas Hendricks
(73) Patrick Henry Herndon, Virginia
(74) William D. Hersee, New York
(75) Tapley Holland, Pennsylvania
(76) Samuel Holland, Pennsylvania
(77) William D. Howell, Massachusetts

(78) William Daniel Jackson, Ireland via Kentucky
(79) Thomas Jackson, Kentucky
(80) Green B. Jamison, Kentucky
(81) Gordon C. Jennings, Missouri
(82) Lewis Johnson, Wales
(83) William Johnson, Pennsylvania
(84) John Jones, New York
(85) Johnny Kellog, Gonzales, Texas
(86) James Kenny, Virginia
(87) Andrew Kent, Kentucky
(88) Joseph Kerr, Louisiana
(89) George C. Kimball, New York, via Gonzales, Texas
(90) William P. King, Gonzales, Texas
(91) John G. King, Gonzales, Texas
(92) William Irvine Lewis, Pennsylvania
(93) William J. Lightfoot, Virginia
(94) Jonathan L. Lindley, Illinois
(95) William Linn, Massachusetts
(96) George Washington Main, Virginia
(97) William T. Malone, Georgia
(98) William Marshall, Tennessee
(99) Albert Martin, Tennessee and Gonzales, Texas
(100) Edward McCafferty, San Patricio, Texas
(101) Jesse McKoy, Gonzales, Texas
(102) William McDowell, Pennsylvania
(103) James McGee, Ireland
(104) John McGregor, Scotland
(105) Robert McKinney, Ireland
(106) Eliel Melton, South Carolina
(107) Thomas R. Miller, Virginia & Gonzales, Texas
(108) William Mills, Tennessee
(109) Isaac Millsaps, Mississippi
(110) Edward F. Mitchusson, Kentucky
(111) Edwin T. Mitchell, Georgia
(112) Napoleon Bonaparte Mitchell, Belvidere, Tennessee
(113) Robert B. Moore, Virginia
(114) Robert Musselman, Ohio
(115) George Neggan, South Carolina
(116) Andrew M. Nelson, Tennessee
(117) Edward Nelson, South Carolina
(118) James Northcross, Virginia
(119) James Nowlin, Ireland
(120) George Pagan, Mississippi
(121) Christopher Parker, Mississippi
(122) William Parks, San Patricio, Texas
(123) Richardson Perry
(124) Amos Pollard, Massachusetts and New York
(125) John Purdy Reynolds, Pennsylvania
(126) Thomas H. Roberts

(127) James Robertson, Tennessee
(128) Isaac Robinson, Scotland
(129) James M. Rose, Virginia, Tennessee
(130) Jackson J. Rusk, Ireland
(131) Joseph Rutherford, Kentucky
(132) Isaac Ryan, Louisiana
(133) Mial Scurlock, Louisiana
(134) Marcus L. Sewell, England
(135) Manson Shied, Georgia
(136) Cleland Kinlock Simmons, North Carolina
(137) Andrew H. Smith, Tennessee
(138) Charles S. Smith, Maryland
(139) Joshua G. Smith, North Carolina & Tennessee
(140) William H. Smith, Nacogdoches, Texas
(141) Richard Starr, England
(142) James E. Stewart, England
(143) Richard L. Stockton, Virginia
(144) A. Spain Summerlin, Tennessee & Arkansas
(145) William E. Summers, Tennessee & Pecan Valley, Texas
(146) William D. Sutherland, Alabama
(147) Edward Taylor, Liberty, Texas
(148) George Taylor, Liberty, Texas
(149) James Taylor, Liberty, Texas
(150) William Taylor, Tennessee
(151) B. Archer M. Thomas, Kentucky
(152) Henry Thomas, Germany
(153) Jesse G. Thompson, North Carolina & Tennessee
(154) John M. Thurston, Pennsylvania & Kentucky
(155) Bruke Trammel, Ireland, via Tennessee
(156) William Barrett Travis, North Carolina & Alabama
(157) George W. Tumlinson, Missouri
(158) Asa Walker, Tennessee
(159) Jacob Walker, Tennessee
(160) William B. Ward, Ireland
(161) Henry Warnell, Arkansas
(162) Joseph G. Washington, Tennessee
(163) Thomas Waters, England
(164) William Wells, Georgia
(165) Isaac White, Kentucky
(166) Robert White, Gonzales, Texas
(167) Hiram J. Williamson, Pennsylvania
(168) David L. Wilson, Scotland
(169) John Wilson, Pennsylvania
(170) Antony Wolfe, England
(171) Clairborne Wright, North Carolina
(172) Charles Zanco
(173) . . . Anderson

INTRODUCTION

"**ALAMO SOLDIER, THE STORY OF PEACE-
FUL MITCHELL**" is the true story of Napoleon
Bonaparte Mitchell, the 17 year old long lean lad from
Belvidere, Tennessee, the only man in the Alamo who
didn't want to kill, didn't believe in violence, or the
taking of a life.

Too little is known of Napoleon Bonaparte Mitchell. History records that he was one of the 13 men in
Davy Crockett's Tennessee Mounted Volunteers who
died defending the "Pallisade" wall of the Alamo.
This was the south wall, between the chapel and the
Guard House, a wall hurriedly built of hides and
poles, after the arrival of General Santa Anna, commander of the 4,000 man Mexican Army.

Napoleon Bonaparte Mitchell insisted on being
called "Peaceful" Mitchell, a nick-name he acquired
when he refused to kill a neighbor who had shot his
father over a boundary dispute, the location of a
"boundary oak tree" locating and separating the
boundary between Mitchell property and Moffett
property on Shaw Mountain near Belvidere, Tennessee.

This is the story of what it was like to be a 17 year
old Tennessean in the Texas Army of 1836.

ALAMO SOLDIER

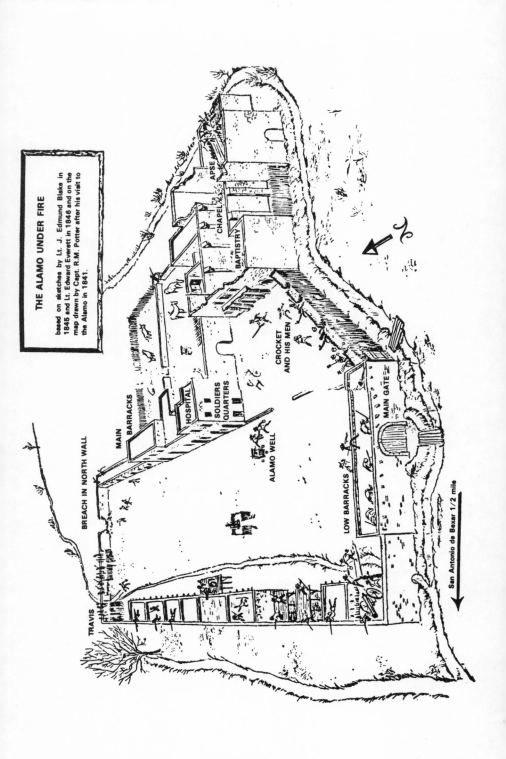

THE ALAMO UNDER FIRE

based on sketches by Lt. J. Edmund Blake in 1845 and Lt. Edward Everett in 1846 and on the map drawn by Capt. R.M. Potter after his visit to the Alamo in 1841.

APSE

CHAPEL

BAPTISTRY

CROCKET AND HIS MEN

MAIN BARRACKS

HOSPITAL

SOLDIERS QUARTERS

ALAMO WELL

MAIN GATE

LOW BARRACKS

BREACH IN NORTH WALL

TRAVIS

San Antonio de Bexar 1/2 mile

1

Napoleon Bonaparte Mitchell had the long lean
limbs of a hungry greyhound, and the thin cheeks
and shaggy rough-cut hair cut of a 17 year old "mountain" boy from southeastern Tennessee. Quiet blue
eyes had the composure of one who had missed many
meals. His long fingers said he had eaten food served
on cornshucks and drank coffee made of roasted black
sweet potato peel instead of coffee beans.

He wore a cheap wide brimmed black hat, but on
this cold January morning in 1836, he had a white
handkerchief made of cotton bed-sheeting pulled
down over his ears and it was tied neatly under his
chin as if tied by female hands to protect his ears. His
yellowed buckskin jacket was three inches shorter in
the sleeves than his wrists; it hadn't grown as fast as
he had. His belt was tanned brown horse-skin, with
the bristly hair still in place. His grey homespun
pants billowed at the knees from long usage.

A grey wool blanket crossed his right shoulder in a
long "U" shaped travel roll, with the "U" on top. His
Kentucky rifle was cradled in his left arm, a shot-bag
of yellow leather and a sharp tipped white cow horn,
serving as his powder-horn, rattled near his horse-
hair belt.

He didn't like his name, preferred his nick-name,
"Peaceful" Mitchell. On his way to Texas, he had
hired out in Hatchez, Mississippi as a wagon-driver,
and was driving a 4-horse covered wagon for a
woman and her two children. His horse, "Old Blue"
jogged behind the wagon, on a short rein, constantly

moving out to the side of the wagon, trying to see around the wagon, to see his master.

Gaines Ferry lay below the red clay hills covered with pines on the border of East Texas. It required several halloows and shouts to call James Gaines out of his house and down to the Sabine River. He waved at them, then stopped at his fire on the east side of his one-room log cabin where his wife was washing clothes. He lifted a coal and lit his pipe, then dropped it back in the fire, wiping his finger to cool it off before he clambered onto the ferry and grabbed the ropes and began pulling the raft across, pulling it through two ringed staves on each end of the upstream side of the raft.

After they crossed the Sabine River and unloaded the wagon from the ferry, Peaceful asked Mr. Gaines, "I've been trying to catch an ex-Congressman from Tennessee by the name of Crockett. Has he been through this way yet?"

"You mean Davy Crockett? Yeah, he's done been through; I ferried him and seven other men." The ferrymen turned to his wife. "Annie, what day was it that tall grinnin' Tennessean—the one in the coon-skin cap—what day was it he came through here?"

"Sakes alive!" Annie Gaines wiped her hands on her apron and moved away from the wash pot. "My heart ain't slowed down since he left here. It's not every day a Congressman comes by, leastwise not a Congressman as handsome as Crockett."

"Why Annie, Governor Sam Houston, he's come through here at least twice that I know of. He was governor of Tennessee."

Annie Gaines waved away his words. "Yeah, but he weren't near as good-looking."

Peaceful interrupted, "Well when did Crockett come through? How far is he ahead of me?"

"Yeah, Annie, what day was it that Crockett came through here?"

"Well, let's see now, my heart ain't quit thumping yet." She smiled slyly. "Must have been three days ago."

2

"Yeah, that Crockett fellow, he's three days ahead of you," Gaines repeated his wife's words.

"Crockett got to Texas before I did." Peaceful stared at the ground unhappily, then looked up at Annie Gaines. "I got kinda stuck on him, too, like you did, Mrs. Gaines. I met him in Memphis on the other side of the Mississippi, and liked being around him. I kinda wanted to make the trip to Texas with him, but he came down the river on a steamboat, and I had to take the Natchez Trace."

"They still using that road?" James Gaines asked with disapproval. "My brother, Pen—most people call him General Pendleton Gaines; he's head of the Louisiana Regular Army—he says the Natchez Trace is dead, nobody travels it any more."

"He's right. Not many people travel the Trace any more—just slaves, Indians, and poor people like me," Peaceful spoke grimly.

"You call yourselves poor folks? Why, you and your wife have got as fine a wagon and team of mules as I ever laid eyes on."

"She ain't my wife," Peaceful spoke before Rosanna Travis turned her bonnetted head.

Rosanna moved toward Mr. Gaines with the three-dollar ferry fare. She raised it high and put it in his outstretched palm. "Mr. Mitchell is a very young 17 year old youngster on his way to Texas. I employed him at Natchez, Mississippi to drive my wagon to take me to my husband in San Augustine, Texas. He's a lawyer there. Have you heard of William B. Travis?"

"Oh yeah!" Gaines pushed back his slouchy hat. "Everybody's head of ole Buck Travis. He's a wild-eyed one, he is. He pretty near started a war with Mexico."

"He what?" Rosanna Travis gasped.

"Yeah, ole Buck Travis, he stole a cannon from a Mexican captain and dared him to come and get it. This was while ole Buck was still at Anhuac. I think that Mexican captain's name was Tenorio. He was he-man of the Mexican garrison at Anhuac. When them

3

Mexicans started after ole Buck's stolen cannon, old Buck lit a fuse light and held it up about hat-high." Gaines reached up and jerked his hat off his head, held it high and slapped it against his leg. "You should've seen them Mexicans scatter. They ran like quail in a hail storm. They was sure lookin' for cover.

"Are you saying my husband is in the Texan Army?" Rosanna Travis asked.

"I wouldn't know, Ma'am. I wouldn't know who is in the army and who ain't in the army. But I will say this, Ma'am. Most everybody in Texas is in the army."

"But my husband's an attorney." Rosanna shook her head. "He's a very capable attorney; he wouldn't be in any army."

"If your husband is Buck Travis, Ma'am," Gaines removed his hat with respect, "he's bound to be in the army. He's got more guts than ere general I've ever seen."

"Oh no! Oh no!" Rosanna Travis raised her parasol and jerked it open unhappily. "He couldn't have. He just couldn't have!" Rosanna closed the umbrella slowly, like a weary soldier at the end of a losing battle. She raised her head slowly and bit her lip as she looked at Peaceful. "We must hurry. We must hurry to San Augustine. I must find my husband. I must find him and talk him into returning to South Carolina. We need him."

"But if he's in the army, Ma'am . . ." Peaceful held her hand as she stepped into the wagon and scooted over on the wagon seat, helping her children up behind her, leaving room for Peaceful to drive.

Rosanna was hiding her face with her hands. Then slowly she lowered her hands and her bonnetted face rose. It showed sudden determination. "I don't care if he is in the army. I'll purchase his discharge."

"Yes, Ma'am," Peaceful flipped the reins, and the mules jerked their heads and surged forward, pulling the wagon up the low red hill away from the Sabine River.

4

At the top of the hill, Peaceful touched Rosanna on the arm, causing her to raise her head slowly and wipe her tears away.

"Ma'am, I was just wonderin' if there was some way I could just trade places with him. I've come all the way to Texas so I could join up. Maybe if he wanted out, they'd let me just take his place."

Rosanna stared at Peaceful with a glum set to her mouth and eyes. She shook her head. "If my husband's joined the army, he'll never want out. He loves a good fight. He particularly likes to be the underdog. If he's in the army, I've made my trip for nothing."

"Oh, I don't think so." Peaceful looked at Little Susan Travis with her tiny bonnet and frilly sleeves. "When your husband sees Little Susan with her shy grin, and 6 year old Charlie here with his freckles and that chaw of tobacco bulging out the side of his jaw," Peaceful reached over and riffled Charles' hair, "he'll hug you and he'll hug them, and then he'll tell that army to hire somebody else to steal tham Mexican cannons."

Charles said, "Her name is Susan Isabella Travis, but Momma calls her "Susan".

Rosanna reached up and wiped the hair out of her face. "Do you think he'll like us? He hasn't seen us in more than three years."

"Yeah, you bet he'll like you. He'll take ole Charlie huntin' a couple o' times and he'll get one hug from Little Susan here." Peaceful lowered the reins a little bit and leaned over toward Little Susan. "Are you gonna hug your daddy around the neck like you have ole Peaceful?"

Little Susan raised her bonnetted head and nodded sweetly.

"I'm gonna join the army with him." Charles leaned forward over the wagon footboard and spat brown tobacco juice on the mule's tail.

"Oh no, I won't have both of my men in that army." Rosanna reached over and put both arms around little Charles and hugged him close. Little Charles didn't even look at his mother; he just looked up at Peaceful and grinned, like he was in a hurry to get to Texas.

When Rosanna finally turned loose of Charles, he turned to Peaceful. "Did my daddy really steal a cannon from them Mexicans?"

"I don't know, Charles. I just know that Mr. Gaines at the ferry said somebody named Buck Travis stole a cannon from a Mexican captain and dared him to come get it."

Charles turned to his mama. "Was that my pa, Mama, was that my pa?"

"Yes, Charles, that sounds very much like your father." Rosanna shaded her eyes from the sun in the western sky, looking for San Augustine behind the hill.

2

"We're a mite suspicious of anybody that comes around here lookin' for Buck Travis." Lonnie Boles pushed back the shoulder straps on his leather blacksmith's apron and gently pounded his smithy's hammer into the palm of his hand. "Most everybody in San Augustine knows the President of Mexico has sent his brother-in-law, General Cos, into San Antonio with five hundred Mexican troupers with specific orders to arrest Travis for treason." He paused, studying Peaceful distrustfully. "General Cos has orders to arrest ole Buck Travis," he pounded his hand with the hammer, "then try him," he pounded his hand, "an' then to hang him in the tallest tree he can find."

"I wish you people would quit calling my husband 'old' Buck Travis. My husband is only twenty-six years old." Rosanna's eyes scolded the suspicious blacksmith.

"Your husband!" Lonnie Boles dropped his smitty's hammer. He stared at Rosanna in wide-eyed amazement. Then his eyes moved to Charles and Susan Isabella Travis clinging to their mother's skirt. He rolled his eyes. "Buck's done told everybody in San Augustine that he's a widower!"

"A widower!" Rosanna gasped, bringing her hand to her mouth, trying to catch the gasped words. She shook her head, then turned to Peaceful, her eyes seeking help, protection from the awful news. "But he's written me. He's written me every month."

7

"Yeah," Lonnie Boles picked up his hammer, "an' he's been writing my sister, Rebecca, a letter or two." Lonnie put the hammer over his shoulder. "Buck Travis's been goin' with Rebecca for more'n a year." He cut a glance at Rosanna and her two children. "I think I see why he didn't ask her to marry."

"Oh no!" Rosanna turned and put her arm over her face while Susan Isabella squeezed her arms around her mother's leg and Charles spat a black stream of tobacco at Lonnie's Bole's dusty boots.

"Mr. Travis seems to like women with an 'r' in their first name," Peaceful tried to say something.

"My husband is a faithful man. He's as faithful as the day is long." Rosanna shifted her shoulders and bent low, comforting her children. "I'm not worried about William Barrett Travis trifling with another woman. He's not that kind of man. He doesn't do things that would make him run." Rosanna suddenly rose to her feet. "That warrant of arrest! Maybe that will help me get him in a wagon headed for South Carolina." She shook her head. "No, that would be running. If I know William Barrett Travis, he is headed for San Antonio to make that Mexican general eat his warrant!" Rosanna smiled at her children. "That's your father. He runs to a fight, but never away from one. Maybe it's good we've come to Texas. At least you'll get to see your father. Susan will get to hug his neck and Charles'll get to go hunting with him." Rosanna looked at her hands. Her eyes said she wondered if she'd get to...

3

Wagon camps began to appear before they reached Nacogdoches; camps located at springs trickling out of the rocky red hills. Women bent over, tending camp fires under wet tarps stretched from the rear of the wagons to nearby trees.

Peaceful saw two men, and as the Travis wagon drew closer, Peaceful looked again and saw they were not ordinary men. They were dressed in military grey with blue stripes down the britches legs. Peaceful turned around in the wagon seat, watching the soldiers in grey cooking their breakfast under a wagon sheet stretched from the rear of an ox cart.

"Soldiers!" Peaceful punched Charles and pointed at the two men, who waved at him, waving their long wooden cooking forks.

"Is that my daddy?" Charles asked.

Peaceful looked at Rosanna. Rosanna looked at him, then looked at Charles. She shook her head. "no, that's not your father." Rosanna shaded her eyes with her hand and stared at the two men disappearing behind the wagon. Then she rose in the wagon seat and took another look. When she sat down, she had a sad face. "I wonder if I will know him." Rosanna put her elbows on her knees and her hand under her chin as she studied the floorboard of the wagon despondently. "Three years is a long time."

Peaceful stopped the wagon at the top of the hill just east of Nacogdoches and dropped the reins as he stared at the lines of men marching three abreast around the tree-shaded square of the small city. A line of mounted cavalry could be seen wheeling and turning, stirring up dust as the horses turned briskly, trying to keep in a line three abreast.

"It's the Texas Army!" Peaceful climbed to the top of the wagon seat for a better look.

"Is that my daddy?" Charles climbed up on the wagon seat beside Peaceful.

Rosanna sat motionless in the wagon seat clinging to her daughter, not looking at the city, not seeing the city. She sat still and immobile with the white face of a woman rejected, her head down with the nervous eyes of a woman who faced another rejection.

They rolled into town slowly, Peaceful turning in his seat to watch each group of men as they marched past.

"Is that my daddy?" Charles pounded Peaceful in the ribs.

Peaceful shrugged his shoulders and turned to Rosanna.

Rosanna shook her head as Charles turned toward her.

"Well, where is my daddy?"

"We'll stop at the Marksman Hotel." Rosanna pointed at the white stone hotel. "I want to check in and pretty up before I look for my husband."

"If I have your permission, Ma'am," Peaceful stopped the wagon at the wooden hitching rack in front of the Marksman Hotel and took off his black hat in a courtesy toward Mrs. Travis, "I'll be untyin' Old Blue from the rear of the wagon and seeking me a place in this Texas Army before dark settles down."

"I employed you, Mr. Mitchell, to take me to my husband. I haven't found him."

"But we're here," Peaceful waved his hand toward the lines of marching men and the dusty cavalry. "This is Nacogdoches; this is where I've come to join the army."

"I want you to stay with me until I find my husband."

10

"But you have Joe." Peaceful pointed to long-armed, slender Joe, Travis' negro slave. "He can help you with your things."

"I'll not pay you until you stand beside me when I speak to my husband."

"Aw, that's alright about the pay, Mrs. Travis. I enjoyed the trip. If any pay was owed, it would be my need to pay you."

"You don't want your pay?"

"I haven't earned any pay." Peaceful pressed his black hat down on his head with both hands, then gave Mrs. Travis a smart salute. He got down on his knees in the street and held his arms out to Little Susan. She ran up and put her arms around his neck and squeezed. Peaceful stuck his hand out and shook hands with Charles. "I hope you don't choke on that chewing tobacco before you find your father." Peaceful reached up and tweaked the yellow cowlick on the side of Charles' head.

"'Twouldn't hurt me if I did." Charles spat a long black stream of tobacco juice at the hitching post.

Peaceful got back to his feet and walked to the rear of the wagon and shook hands with Joe. "Joe, now you take care of Mrs. Travis, an' if you run into any problem, anything that I can help with, you come to me an' I'll help in every way I can."

"Yes, Sir, Mr. Mitchell. If ole Joe ever needs a friend, he'll call on you."

Peaceful turned to wave good-bye to Mrs. Travis, but she held out her hand toward him. "Peaceful," she waved her hand for him to come toward her, "I can't let you leave without your pay."

"I don't need pay, Mrs. Travis. I'll be in the army tonight or the first thing in the morning."

"I want you to do me one more favor," Rosanna asked.

Peaceful walked toward Mrs. Travis and pressed down on his hat again as if he were in a hurry to leave. "Yes, Ma'am." Peaceful released his hat and lowered his hands with resignation.

11

"I want you to be with me when I meet my husband."

"When you meet your husband!" Peaceful stepped backward.

"In case he should decide to return with us to South Carolina, if you were there, you could tell him that you would volunteer to take his place."

Peaceful stared at Joe, who was staring at him from the rear of the wagon. "Well, I don't know." Peaceful rubbed his jaw thoughtfully. "I don't wanna take nobody's place; I just wanna join up!"

"My husband may be a captain. They say he almost started this war with Mexico single-handedly."

"Yeah, an' if I took his place, I might be hung by General Santa Anna instead of him."

Peaceful walked to the rear of the wagon and began untying Old Blue. Peaceful had just untied his laso from the rear of the wagon and was holding the reins in his hands when he heard a gasp.

"Oh my God!" Rosanna was standing at the side of the wagon when she gasped and dropped her black parasol. Peaceful turned and looked at Rosanna. He saw she had her arms raised and stood stiff and white-faced. She held her hands out slowly in front of her and walked toward a man approaching from the other side of the street. He stopped suddenly and held up both hands.

"Rosanna, what on God's earth are you doing here!"

"William B. Travis!" Rosanna held out her hands and reached for her husband.

4

William B. Travis stood in the middle of the street with his hands held up, pushing them away from him as if to ward off an unwanted thing, but Rosanna's arms circled around his smart military grey uniform. She shook him, rattling the sword slung from his belt. She clung to his waist. Her head rose slowly, coming to the top of his shoulders.

Rosanna stepped one step back and placed her arms around his neck. "I've come for my husband." She shook her head, drinking in his bronze tanned face, even white teeth, and his proud blue eyes. She moved her lips toward his, seeking his lips in a wifely embrace.

Travis stepped backward, pushing her away from him. "But Rosanna, not here." Travis took off his military grey hat and wiped the sweat from his brow with the sleeve of his military jacket. "I must talk to you in private."

Little Charles stepped forward to the front of the wagon with a cud of tobacco jutting out the side of his jaw. "Is that my daddy?" He pointed his little hand over the wagon seat at William B. Travis, but he was looking at Joe, Travis' slave.

Joe nodded his head. "Yes, Sir, Mr. Charles, that's your daddy."

Charles lowered his hand slowly, blinking his eyes, just looking, rolling his head slightly, not knowing what he should do.

William B. Travis stepped around Rosanna. "Charles! Charles! My Little Charles!" He ran toward his son with his hands outstretched. He pulled Little Charles from the wagon and dropped to his knees, circling his arms around his son. Little Charles bent his head in a one-eyed frown, shutting one eye and looking over his father's shoulder, studying his mother, with his other eye, looking at her, seeking her approval. She was dabbing her eyes with a white handkerchief.

"And this must be Susan." William Travis reached out with one arm, but Susan didn't move to him. She stayed in the shade of the wagon sheet, blinking her big blue eyes, sucking her thumb, stepping back slightly to get away from her father's grasp.

Rosanna walked over and lifted her daughter out of the wagon seat and patted her gently, while Little Susan put her arms around her mother's neck and squeezed her tightly. She turned her blue eyes to the man who had reached for her with his long arm. Susan looked at him for a fearful blue-eyed second. Then she turned and squeezed her mother again and whispered, "I want my mama."

When Travis rose from his knees, he had Charles in his arms. Charles was looking at his father with a quizzical look. Finally he reached over and ran his finger along his father's chin. "I think you need a shave."

"Yes, let's check into the hotel." Rosanna waved her arms for Joe to bring their things. She turned and looked at her husband. "Maybe we can find the privacy you need after we get checked in."

Peaceful raised his hand to his hat. "Will you be needing me, Mrs. Travis?" Peaceful saluted.

"Oh." Rosanna stopped. "I owe Mr. Mitchell $25.00 for escorting us through Louisiana." Rosanna nodded her head toward Peaceful Mitchell.

"Peaceful Mitchell's my name." Peaceful stepped forward and shook hands with Colonel William B. Travis. "It was a pleasure riding through Louisiana with your family."

"Oh, ah, er ah." Travis reached inside of his jacket as if he were reaching for his billfold. "I'm sorry, Rosanna, but I haven't been paid."

"I am the one that employed him; I am the one who should pay him." Rosanna stepped toward the wagon and reached for her purse.

Peaceful stepped backward. "I'm sorry, Mrs. Travis, but I can't accept pay for the pleasure of riding through Louisiana with your fine little family." Peaceful shook his head. "I know you said you would pay me for guiding you through Louisiana," Peaceful smiled, "but you know who did the guiding; it was you, not me. I will accept no pay for such a pleasant trip." Rosanna offered a $25.00 gold nugget from her yellow leather purse to Peaceful, but he shook his head. "I could never accept pay from a lady who cooks as good as you do, Mrs. Travis." Peaceful pushed away the offered coin.

"How many days did it take you to cross Louisiana?" Travis asked, as Joe began handing down parcels and packages from the wagon.

"Was it eleven or twelve days?" Peaceful asked Rosanna as he helped set the parcels on the wooden board walk in front of the hotel.

"It took twelve. We went through Winnsboro." Rosanna smiled at her husband.

"Did you have any trouble?" Travis asked Peaceful.

"No trouble; just cholera."

"Cholera!" Travis gasped and turned and looked at his six-year-old son.

"I kept your children in the wagon for three days and nights." Rosanna reached up and took her round handbag as it was being handed down from the wagon by Joe. "I never let your children touch ground or drink unboiled water until we got through the cholera country. We travelled fast until we got ahead of the slaves and left the cholera behind us." She handed her bag to William Travis. "If you don't mind, William, I'd like for Mr. Mitchell to accompany us into the privacy of this hotel."

15

"Huh?" Peaceful and William Travis spoke at the same time.

"I want Mr. Mitchell to be present when you tell me whether or not you are returning to South Carolina with your family."

William Travis set the suitcase down. He didn't set Charles down, but kept him curled in his left arm. He looked at Charles, then turned to his wife. "I can't leave Texas. I have been commissioned as an officer in the Texas Army. I damn near started this war. I can't leave now."

"I thought you wanted to talk about this in the privacy of a hotel room." Rosanna folded her arms across her chest.

"I wanted to talk about you and me in the privacy of a hotel room." He turned and stared at Peaceful Mitchell with disapproval. "And I don't need Mr. Mitchell's company at a family discussion."

"Mr. Mitchell's come to join the army," Rosanna Travis hastened her words.

William Travis looked at Peaceful's long slender body and slouchy black hat. Travis shook his head and picked up the suitcase.

"I'm just gonna join as a private," Peaceful volunteered quickly.

"You gonna join the Volunteer or the Regulars?" Travis asked as he started into the Marksman Hotel with Charles in one arm and the heavy yellow leather suitcase in the other hand.

Peaceful shrugged his shoulders. "What's the difference?"

"Volunteers can quit when they want to; Regulars have to stay until the fighting is over." William B. Travis opened the hotel door and motioned for Peaceful to enter, but Peaceful shook his head and remained outside the hotel.

"I came to join whichever outfit will have me."

"You sound like Crockett and his Tennessee Mounted Volunteers." Travis set his suitcase down and remained outside the hotel door with Peaceful.

"Is Davy Crockett already here?" Peaceful asked.

16

"Yeah, you'll find his outfit in some white tents camped under some Spanish oaks on the west side of town, on the King's Highway about half a mile southwest of town."

"Thank you, Sir." Peaceful saluted Colonel William B. Travis. He turned and saluted Mrs. Travis. "If you will excuse me, Ma'am, me an' Ole Blue will be moseying on down toward them Spanish oaks and seein' if Crockett's got room for another Tennessee volunteer."

Rosanna set her parcels down and walked over and put both her hands around Peaceful's hands. "You're a fine young man, Peaceful Mitchell, I wish you'd let me pay you." She shook Peaceful's hands.

Peaceful shook his head.

"I wish I could find someone like you to escort me back to South Carolina."

"Do you think you'll have to go?"

Rosanna nodded her head. "I've known it ever since I crossed the Sabine River. My husband doesn't want to raise cotton, corn, and tobacco. He was born to be a leader of men. I shall have to give him to Texas." She looked at William B. Travis. He looked at Rosanna. He clenched his jaw and stared at the yellow suitcase.

5

There weren't any men in the two white tents.
Peaceful pushed back the flap of the tent and stole a
quick look. The first tent had five blanket beds on the
ground underlaid with buffalo skin. The one nearest
the door had a pack saddle for a pillow. The two tents
faced each other, so it was no trouble for Peaceful to
glance around and open the flap of the second tent. It,
too, was empty. It was a much longer tent with six
bunks, all on the ground with neat grey blankets on
top of black bearskin bedrolls. A round table made of
a three-foot thick sawed off log was set in the center of
the tent. It contained two brown whiskey jugs, a deck
of red cards, and a green candle, burned nearly to the
bottom, spreading its green wax over the top of the
sawed-off log table.

Outside the tent, Peaceful stuck one finger into the
ashes to see how warm it was and he felt coals.
He busied himself blowing away the ashes and blowing the coals back to life. He gathered wood and got
the fire back to crackling with a good bright yellow
flame.

Peaceful was standing at the fire warming his
hands when he heard the thunder of horse hooves and
shouts followed by Tennessee curses.

Peaceful spotted Crockett in his coonskin cap leaning forward in his saddle flipping his reins.

"Last man in camp has to cook supper," Crockett
shouted, as the racing horses neared the two tents
and the lonely campfire.

Crockett led the way, and as he passed the fire, he raised in his saddle, staring at Peaceful as he raced past. He turned his horse and led it back to camp, heaving and tossing its head, with steam rising from the shoulders and neck.

"I beat 'em, didn't I?" Crockett shouted as he dismounted. "I beat 'em fair and square, and I didn't have more'n ten yards' head start." He turned and grinned as the horses heaved and snorted white steam as they came into camp. "Little Joe's gonna have to wash dishes," Crockett laughed. "Ole Joe Bayliss'll have to fry steak and taters tonight."

"You cheat, Colonel Crockett," Joseph Bayliss accused. "You didn't call the terms of the race until you was already nearly in camp." Bayliss pushed up the front of his white hat. "I can beat you at cards, even if I can't beat you racing." Little Joe Bayliss climbed off his horse. Then he saw Peaceful near the fire. Peaceful was reaching out and taking the horses' reins as they came into camp. "Looks like you not only have won a race, but maybe another recruit," Bayliss commented.

"Yes, Sir." Peaceful reached out and took the reins of Crockett's horse. "I hurried to Texas as fast as I could, but I couldn't catch Davy Crockett," Peaceful grinned. "I'd be obliged if you let me stake out your horses. Where do you keep your stake pins?" Peaceful extended his right hand toward Crockett. "My name's Napoleon Bonaparte Mitchell, but I'd be proud if you'd call me Peaceful Mitchell."

"Glad to meet you, Mr. Mitchell." Crockett shook hands with Peaceful. "You'll find the stake pins just inside the tent." Crockett nodded his head at Peaceful. "We'd be much obliged if you take supper with us."

Peaceful had started toward the tent, but he stopped and turned around. "I've come to join up, Mr. Crockett. I'd like to join up with your outfit."

"Well, you'll have to be voted in." Crockett put on a serious face.

Peaceful looked at the men gathering around Crockett.

Suddenly the little man with a pushed-up brim on his hat popped Crockett on the shoulder with a lusty blow. "Don't let the colonel kid you. Ain't none of us joined yet. We're supposed to enlist tommorrow."

"You think I have a chance of joining up with your Volunteers?"

"You will have to be voted on, and of course, we can't vote til after you cook supper for us," Crockett grinned.

"Yes, Sir." Peaceful gathered up the reins of the five horses. "I'll stake these horses out, then come back and see what I can rustle up for supper."

When Peaceful came back to camp, Crockett was waiting. "Mr. Mitchell, I'd like you to meet Little Joe Bayliss, the best poker player that ever got run out of Tennessee on a rail." Crockett slapped Joseph Bayliss on the shoulder. "We call him Little Joe Bayliss."

"Glad to meet you, Mr. Bayliss." Peaceful shook his hand.

"This here is Robert Campbell, but nobody calls him Campbell. Everybody calls him Cherokee because he's part Indian and he's proud of it."

Peaceful shook hands with dark-skinned, dark-haired Cherokee Campbell.

"Don't talk about Indians around me," Campbell warned, "or I'll scalp you in my sleep. I got more Cherokee blood than I have Scotch."

"I'm glad to meet you, Mr. Campbell."

"Just call me Cherokee." Cherokee Campbell patted Peaceful on the shoulder.

"This here's Squire Daymon," Crockett introduced a stocky thick-set red-faced man with red hair and a red bandana kerchief around his neck. "Don't ever Indian wrestle ole Squire; he'll throw your butt."

"Glad to meet you, Mr. Daymon." Peaceful shook hands with the stocky red-faced man. Peaceful suddenly leaned forward, feeling power and strength in the grip of Squire Daymon's hand. "I like to wrestle. I'll be looking to taking you on in a little wrestling match." Peaceful winced as he felt the man bear down with all his might on Peaceful's hand. He kept his composure and squeezed right back. "I especially like Indian wrestling."

"I'll take you on right after supper," Squire Daymon growled.

"This here is Johnny M. Hays, the best chicken picker that ever saw a chicken house." Crockett introduced a tall slender young man with close-cropped blonde hair.

"Aw, Colonel, you know I'm a forager, I forage food for my men, I don't steal chickens; I just find 'em." Johnny Hays shook hands with Peaceful. "I just find chickens where folks has caught 'em and wrung their necks and then dropped 'em."

"There's six more wild-uns from Tennessee gonna be ridin' up here in a few minutes." Crockett put his arm around Peaceful and led him toward the tent. "They've gone to the woods to get us a wild turkey or two. We better get that skillet out and get it hot, 'cause they'll be here in a few minutes."

"How long you been here, Congressman Crockett? How long you been in Nacogdoches?" Peaceful asked.

"I've been here since January the fifth. I came to Texas the long way, through Arkansas. I crossed the Red River at Fulton, then I headed southeast through Clarksville. I ran out of money at Lost Prairie. I mean I ran plum out. But I come across this fellow Issac Jones. He had a silver watch, and he kinda took a fancy to my gold one, so I traded watches with him for $30.00 boot. He tried to trade me outta my rifle, Old Betsy, but ole Davy Crockett ain't never gonna get hungry enough to trade off Old Betsy. She was given to me for something courageous I was supposed to have done when I was in Congress. See this inscription? All the way down the barrell. Just read that."

"Presented by the young men of Philadelphia to the Honorable David Crockett."

Peaceful ran his fingers down the inscription on the barrell. "I ain't never been given nothing, nothing much, but I understand that when you are given something, it becomes something special that you can't sell or trade away."

"Yeah, when I go, I hope they bury Old Betsy right beside me," Crockett sighed.

"Here comes Jim Ewing," Little Joe ran to the edge of the tent for a better view of the road. "Look at him wave them wild turkey."

"I'm so hungry I almost ate 'em raw," Jim Ewing shouted as he vaulted off his horse.

"Where's the rest of the boys?" Crockett asked.

"Aw, they had to drop by the commissary and draw a jug of whiskey." Ewing handed the turkeys to Squire Daymon and walked over and warmed his hands at the fire. He was standing by the fire when he spied Peaceful. "Who's this?"

Peaceful walked toward him with his hand outstretched. "I'm Peaceful Mitchell." Peaceful stuck out his hand.

"What!" Ewing shook hands with Peaceful and laughed. "What's a man with a name like that doing in an army camp like this?"

Crockett broke in. "His name's Napoleon Bonaparte Mitchell. He said he adopted the nickname Peaceful so he wouldn't have to fight everybody he met."

"Well, that sounds like a pretty damn good reason." Ewing shook hands with Peaceful. "Where you from, Mr. Mitchell?" Ewing asked.

"I'm from Shaw Mountain near Belvidere, Tennessee."

"Well, Andy Nelson's from Bean's Creek. I think that's not far from Belvidere."

"Bean's Creek! That's where I went to church," Peaceful said. "Where's this Nelson at?"

"Aw he's over there at the commissary cabins gettin' some whiskey."

"That word whiskey sounds like somebody from Bean's Creek."

Andy Nelson's horse bounced hams and whiskey jugs as he rode into camp. Peaceful watched as the hams and whiskey crocks were carefully untied from the saddle.

Andy Nelson and Crockett talked and pointed at Peaceful. Then Andy Nelson walked toward Peaceful and stuck out his hand for a handshake.

"Colonel Crockett was telling me you're from near Belvidere back in good ole Tennessee." Nelson slapped Peaceful on the shoulder.

"Yeah, I live up the hill a ways from Belvidere, up on Shaw Mountain."

"Shaw Mountain!" Andy Nelson looked at the ground for an instant. "I know where Shaw Mountain is. Don't you go up Bean's Creek til you get to Moffitt's place? Don't that mountain belong to Moffitt now? Didn't he marry Alice Shaw?"

Peaceful nodded his head.

"Did ya ever know any of the Moffitts?"

Peaceful nodded his head again. "My pa bought a piece of land up on the saddleback, almost at the top of Shaw Mountain. We have a little apple orchard where the spring runs out of a crack in the limestone."

"You say your name is Mitchell?" Nelson studied Peaceful as he scratched his ear.

Peaceful nodded.

"Didn't Abner Moffitt kill a fellow by the name of Mitchell up on Shaw Mountain?"

Peaceful studied Andy Nelson silently and finally licked his lips. He nodded his head. "Yeah, that was my pa."

"That's bad." Andy Nelson shook his head. "I hear tell that they was arguin' over a boundary line — the location of a boundary oak — which oak tree was the boundary oak."

Peaceful nodded.

"Your Pa sawed down the oak that gave him the most land."

"He was sawin' it down when he got shot."

"Oh!" Nelson stepped back and waved his arms, "Was you there?"

Peaceful nodded. He looked down, then sighed and raised his head. "I was there."

"I hear your Ma told you to go shoot Abner Moffit, the guy what shot your pa."

Peaceful glanced around him. Finally he nodded.

"And you refused to shoot him." Nelson pointed an accusing hand.

"I told my Ma that if thu Lord wanted Abner Moffit punished, HE would see he was punished."

"Ummm." Nelson licked his lips. "Moffit sure got punished. His pretty daughter died suddenly, the next day, like as if she had been poisoned."

Peaceful Mitchell glared at Andy Nelson, then his anger melted. He shut both eyes. He slumped like a wounded bird. He turned and walked slowly away like a bird dragging a crippled wing.

Peaceful walked away from the camp, toward a gnarled old oak tree down the road a short distance. He reached for the old oak and put his arms around it, hugging it, and stayed there a long time.

Johnny Hays walked around the campfire a couple of times, raising his head from time to time to see if Peaceful was still hugging the gnarled motherly old oak. Hays threw a piece of wood on the fire and walked toward Peaceful and the oak tree. He stopped and watched the youngster leaning against the tree, then, he spoke.

"You an' this Molly Moffit, the girl that died, you wuz sweethearts?" Johnny Hays asked.

Peaceful raised his arms slowly and glanced behind him and when he saw Johnny Hays he lowered his arms, wiped the bark off, and turned and faced Hays. "Don't know about sweethearts." Peaceful leaned back and touched the tree as she spoke. "She lived down the mountain aways. Her folks allus looked down on us 'cause we wuz so poor, tryin' to scratch corn an' taters an' beans out of gravelly mountain soil. Sometimes when I brought cane down to the Moffit place to be squeezed into molasses, I'd sit on thu porch swing and talk. Sometimes when we'd go to Camp Meetin' she'd get off their wagon an' walk with

24

me. We'd hold hands."

"Hold hands!" Johnny Hays threw up his hands in utter disbelief. "Hold hands!" he scowled. "That all you did!"

Peaceful stood still and watched Johnny Hays wiggle and flop his hands and arms. When Hays settled down and got still, Peaceful went on. "Molly Moffit's eyes said she liked me. Her big blue eyes said more in one look than any woman said to you in your whole life."

Johnny Hays shrugged. "Never looked at no woman's eyes."

The next day as they were being sworn in as soldiers in the Texas Army by Judge Forbes on the south side of the square in Nacogdoches, Crockett suddenly interrupted the swearing-in ceremony.

"Hold on now." Crockett held up his hand. "I will not take an oath to defend any government that may be formed as the government of Texas."

"How's that?" Judge Forbes asked.

"I refuse to take an oath of allegiance to any form of government that may be formed. The only government that I will serve will be a democratic republican form of government."

"With your permission, Congressman Crockett, I will change the oath to 'that you will defend any republican form of government that may be created by the Republic of Texas."

"You go right ahead. I'll take that oath and never look back" Crockett said.

Peaceful held up his right hand while the oath was being administered. When it was all over and they were riding back to camp, he asked Crockett, "Does that mean I'm in the Army?"

"Yep, you shore are," Crockett answered.

"You mean that's all there is to it—just holding up your hand?"

"Yeah, that's all there is to it, but let me tell you this, son. You can be shot if you desert or leave, or if you refuse to fight."

"Colonel, you know I'm a man from Tennessee. I won't ever refuse to —" Peaceful licked his lips, "I'll do whatever I'm ordered to do."

6

On January the tenth, 1836, Peaceful met Colonel
Travis at the commissary when Peaceful went there
to draw his provisions for the trip to San Antonio,
where he had been posted along with Crockett and the
eleven other men of Crockett's Mounted Tennessee
Volunteers.

"How are you, Colonel Travis?" Peaceful saluted.

"Just fine." Travis returned the salute. "I hear you
have been posted to San Antonio to the Alamo," Travis commented grufly from behind his desk.

"Yes, Sir, I'm leaving with Colonel Crockett in the
morning."

"I'm posted to San Antonio, too. I'll be leaving here
on the twenty-third. I'd be leaving sooner, but I have
some family matters to attend to."

"Begging your pardon, Sir, but are you and your
wife getting a divorce?"

"Yes. We're getting our divorce on the twenty-first,
and I'll be leaving on the twenty-third."

"Who's getting Little Susie and who's getting
Charles?"

"Rosanna's taking Susie, and I'm taking Charles."

"Are you taking Charles to the Alamo?" Peaceful
asked.

"No, I have a friend named Rebecca. She will keep
Charles until we put this Mexican Army in its proper
place."

"Will you see Mrs. Travis before you leave?" Peaceful asked.

"Yes, I'll see her."

"Will you give my respects to Mrs. Travis, little Susie and your son, Charles?"

"I will give your respects to my children." William Barret Travis huffed. "I won't be saying anything to my wife."

Peaceful stood and stared at Colonel Travis for a long uncomfortable instant. "Yes sir." Peaceful saluted and started to turn.

"One minute." Colonel Travis stopped Peaceful with his young but sharp, authoratative voice. He reached up and wiggled the handkerchief now tied around Peaceful's neck. Travis wrinkled his lips with disapproval. "Why do you always wear that handkerchief? One day you wear it over your head, around your ears, then the next day it swirls around your neck?"

Peaceful reached up and felt of the kerchief knot just under his chin. He felt of the knot without looking at the kerchief.

"It's most unsoldierly looking." Travis sniffed.

Peaceful fondled the knot. A far-away glance rose in his eyes. "That handkerchief knot was tied under my chin by a girl back in Tennessee, a long time ago. I'll never untie the knot. I wear it as close to my heart as I can wear a handkerchief."

"But it's unsoldierly looking. A handkerchief!" Travis shook his head.

"I wash it every once in a while." Peaceful grasped the knot protectively. "I just ain't never gonna un-tie the knot. I ain't never gonna let it get very far away from..."

"Your heart." Colonel Travis let his face break into an understanding smile.

"It's the only thing my Tennessee girl ever gave me, a knot in my handkerchief."

When Peaceful got back to camp, he came on Colonel Crockett loading pack saddles on their horses just outside the tent.

"I just left Colonel Travis at the commissary. He sure was out of snuff."

"Yeah, he just heard that Sam Houston was made general of the Texas Army by Governor Smith down at the capital, Washington-on-the-Brazos. I don't think he's yet quite recovered from the shock of finding out he's not gonna be commander of the Texas Army?"

"I understand he perty near started this war all by himself," Peaceful commented.

"Yeah, those that start a war can seldom end it." Crockett tightened the straps on the last pack saddle.

"I hear we're going by Washington-on-the-Brazos on our way to San Antonio," Peaceful commented.

"Yeah, I've gotta go by the capital and get my rank confirmed. Right now I don't know what my rank is. It's somewhere between a private and colonel," Crockett laughed.

"What'll I call you, Sir? Private Crockett, or Colonel Crockett?"

"Call me Davy Crockett."

Two days after enlistment, there was a general parade of the troops at Nacogdoches being reviewed by General Sam Houston. The first group consisted of Major Ward's Georgia Battalion, followed by Captain Duval's Kentucky Mustangs, a colorful cavalry group on red horses, parading with shiny swords held at right dress as they marched past. They were followed by Captain Burke's Mobile Greys. Next came Captain Shackleford's Red Rovers of Alabama. The last and smallest group consisted of Davy Crockett and his twelve Tennessee Mounted Volunteers, all dressed in buckskin, waving their long Kentucky rifles as they raced by the reviewing stand at the south side of the square in Nacogdoches.

7

"Colonel Crockett, it looks like it's gonna rain all night." Little Joy Bayliss raised high in his stirrups, pointing at a line of low black clouds storming in from the northwest.

"Yeah, it looks like we're going to be in for a cold wet spell." Crockett shaded his eyes with one hand, watching a bolt of lightning sear across the sky and sparkle down a huge oak tree.

All thirteen horses skitted a bit away from the sliver of lightning. The pack horses bucked and Peaceful had to crawl off and settle them down.

"It's gonna be a bad night for campin' out." Cherokee Campbell reached over and patted his horse on the shoulder, watching the tiny white stream of steam rising from the trunk of the lightning-struck oak tree. "That lightning's gonna drive these horses crazy. They'll break their stake ropes and they'll pull up their stake pins. They'll run all night. As long as there's any lightning, they'll not stop to graze."

"Yeah, we need a barn, someplace to pen our horses to keep them from running from the lightning," Crockett agreed.

"Yeah,

"Hey, I see smoke ahead." Little Joe Bayliss pointed at a tiny rising column of dark smoke. "Either lightening struck a tree and set it on fire or there's a cabin in that valley."

"Yeah, and maybe they've got a barn." Peaceful Mitchell spurred Ole Blue.

30

Davy Crockett's thirteen-man company of Tennessee Mounted Volunteers galloped into the Pecan Creek Valley of the Trinity River.

When they rounded a bend in the creek and saw the little cabin and big barn, Crockett grinned as the rain beat down. "Must be a German who built this place. A little house and a big barn. That always means there's a Dutchman around somewhere," Crockett commented. Chickens and pigs scurried before the horses as they galloped into the grassy yard. "Y'all go on to the barn; I'll go stop at the house and get permission and provisions," Crockett shouted as he waved his arm, trying to make his words carry over the thunder and lightning.

Suddenly in the twilight of the approaching storm, the figure of a woman in black stepped out of the door of the cabin. She had a gun and she brought it slowly to her shoulder, and even above the clatter of horses' hooves, Peaceful could hear the click of her pulling the hammer back.

Colonel Crockett's arm rose at once for the men to halt. Even in the shower, a storm of dust followed the horses as they came to a sudden halt.

Peaceful saw the lady in black on the front porch with a gun at her shoulder, and a little cotton-headed boy not a day over ten years old holding a rifle from his perch right behind the back wall of the cabin. Peaceful could see the rifle was too heavy for the little boy. The barrel was rolling and wobbling.

"Who are you and what do you want?" the woman shouted.

Crockett held both arms in the air, one arm to stop his men, and the other arm to stop the woman from shooting. Crockett lowered one arm slowly, took off his coonskin cap, and bowed his head gently. "Colonel Davy Crockett at your services, Ma'am." Crockett waved his arm at the dozen men sitting on their nervous horses. "This is my company of Tennessee Mounted Volunteers. We enlisted in the Texas Army two days ago, and we're on our way to **Washington-on-the-Brazos, the capital of Texas. We'd** appreciate it very much, Ma'am, if you'd let us keep our horses in your barn till after this storm passes. This lightning is giving our horses fits."

The lady turned her head toward her cotton-headed son at the other end of the cabin. "Whatd'ya think, Billy?"

"Well, they don't look like soldiers to me. They look like redlanders." Little Billy's rifle barrel began wobbling something awful. At one time or another he pointed it at every man in the thirteen-man company. Peaceful and everybody else was watching the boy with the rifle that wobbled.

Crockett dismounted and hung his coonskin cap on the pommel of his saddle. He reached inside his buckskin jacket for the paper commissioning him a colonel in the Texas Army and posting him to the Alamo in San Antonio. "We're sure not redlanders, Ma'am. We're gentlemen from Tennessee. I'd like you to examine my commission paper" he held the paper out in front of him, turning it over to protect it from the rain.

"I can't read." The lady lowered her rifle and stared at the white parchment paper. She eyed the paper with respect, then she turned her head to Billy. "Whatd-ya think, Billy?"

"Well, they don't act like no redlanders." The rain suddenly came down harder. "And besides, Mom, it's gettin' awful wet out here. Let's let 'em use the barn." Little Billy lowered his rifle with a sigh and began rubbin his arm where it had got so tired.

"Alright, Billy Boy, you take 'em out to the barn and show 'em where to put their horses." The lady lowered her rifle.

Billy nodded his head and took off in a trot toward the barn, waving his arm for the horses to follow behind him.

"Colonel Crockett, I'm Bertha Summers." The lady in black shifted her rifle to her left hand and stuck out her right hand, shaking hands with Davy Crockett. "I'd be mighty obliged if you would accept a bit of our Texas hospitality and take supper with us." She motioned for Crockett to follow her into the cabin.

Crockett ducked his head as he went through the low door of the cabin. Once inside the cabin, he shook the water from his cap and stomped his boots on a welcome mat made of braided corn shucks. Crocket turned to Bertha Summers. "I'd like to meet the man of the house. Is Mr. Summers about?"

"I speck Mr. Summers is dead. He's either been killed by Indians or he's run away. He's been gone for four months now."

"Oh, I'm sorry, Mrs. Summers." Davy Crockett spoke as he closed the cabin door.

Peaceful had waited outside the cabin holding Crockett's horse, but the rain was now coming down so hard that he turned and led the two horses to the barn.

In a few minutes Crockett came down to the barn. He ran through the rain and burst through the door in a puddle of mud. He paused to swish the water off his cap and off the shoulders of his buckskin jacket. Then he turned and stared at his men. "Mrs. Summers has given us permission to stay in the barn. But she says we can't cook in here or make a fire. She doesn't even want a lamp lit or lantern or a candle. She's afraid we'll catch her barn on fire and burn it up."

"Well, what're we gonna do for supper?" barrel-chested Squire Daymon grumped.

Crockett folded his arms across his chest and leaned back against the barn door, a smile slowly warming his lips. "Mrs. Summers is a very loyal Texas lady. She's gonna fix both supper and breakfast for us. She says she don't want us cookin' around her barn."

"Well if she cooks for us, she'll make a commissary requisition for it, and she'll get paid for it." Little Joe Bayliss walked around the rear of his horse and pointed his finger at Crockett.

"She's a widow, Little Joe," Crockett spoke sharp and fast, stopping Bayliss in his tracks. "She ain't got no man."

"Oh." Little Joe came to a sudden stop and glanced around apologetically. "I didn't know."

"I think it's a good idea to let her feed us and earn an honest buck or two." Crockett jumped forward as a bolt of lightning struck, causing all the horses to bolt and nicker and tremble. After the horses were settled down, Crockett continued. "Mrs. Summers said she'd feed us four at a time. Who's gonna be in that first four?"

Everybody in the barn held up his hand.

Crockett laughed and shook his head and raised his hand, waving all the hands down. "I'll just take the skinniest ones first." Crockett turned aside, waving away any attempt to voice opposition. "Little Joe, you and Peaceful and Cherokee can eat with me." He turned and opened the door of the barn and ran to the cabin.

Peaceful hadn't much more than got in the door of the cabin when Mrs. Summer grabed him by the lapel of his jacket and almost turned him around. "One of you boys go out there and wring the necks of four chickens and bring in one of them baby pigs. There ain't a bite of meat in this house. Fact is, I ain't got nothin' in this house but cornmeal and lard." Peaceful looked at Crockett for a second, but Mrs. Summers didn't take orders from anybody. She pushed Peaceful out the door. "Bring in that pig dead." Mrs. Summers slammed the cabin door shut.

Peaceful stood outside the door in the rain. He slowly opened the door and stuck his head back in. "I can't wring a chicken's neck," Peaceful complained through the open door.

"You go wring those chickens' necks and bring me in a pig, and you knock him in the head before you bring him in here." Mrs. Summers slammed the door on Peaceful's fingers.

Peaceful stood outside the door in the rain for another second or two, then he opened the door again. This time he didn't just stick his head in the door. He walked in and shut the door behind him, holding the door latch in his hands behind his back.

34

He glanced at Colonel Crockett. "Colonel, you'll have to get somebody else to wring them chickens' necks. I just can't do it."

Crockett laughed. "Mrs. Summers, you sent the wrong person to wring them chickens' necks. Peaceful Mitchell can't kill any tame animal; he has a hard time killing a wild one. We've got a chicken eater here who'd really enjoy wringing your chickens' necks." Crockett looked at Cherokee. "Cherokee, you go trade places with Johnny Hays. Tell him to wring four chickens' necks and bring 'em in here. You'll have to trade places with Johnny and take his place in the barn." Crockett turned his attention to Little Joe Bayliss. "Little Joe, you'll have to go catch a pig and cut his throat and gut him, and bring him in here after you've got him all cleaned up and ready to cook." Crockett then turned to Mrs. Summers. "Ma'am is there anything else we can do for you?"

"Well if you have any salt, that would help. We don't have any salt at all."

"Oh, well that." Crockett pointed his finger at Peaceful. "Peaceful, you go out there and get in that mess pack of mine and bring out that box of salt."

Peaceful was glad to leave, glad to get out of the embarrassment of being unable to even kill a chicken. He wondered what Crockett thought of him, and what the men would think whenever they heard that he said he was unable to kill a chicken. Peaceful noticed that this didn't seem to surprise Crockett at all. Maybe that was why he had been appointed colonel. Maybe Crockett could understand why a man could come all the way from Tennessee to Texas to join the army, and yet couldn't kill a chicken. Crockett wouldn't tell on Peaceful, but Peaceful knew Little Joe Bayliss was just waiting for the opportunity to tell and then laugh.

Peaceful didn't pay any attention to the rain at all as he walked to the barn, but when he got to the barn door, he kicked it so hard that the two men inside the barn who were leaning against the door got knocked against the horses. Peaceful whispered to himself, "If

Little Joe tells on me, I'll whup him."

Peaceful couldn't see a thing inside the barn. It was dark as pitch. He groped his way to the horses. "Where's Crockett's horse? He says he's got some salt in his pack."

Salt! What's that lady gonna do, feed us salt crackers?" Squire Daymon laughed.

Peaceful pushed his way to Crockett's horse and felt in the saddlebags for the box of salt, feeling the horse tremble and shake as lightning bolts continued to shake the barn rafters. When Peaceful finally pulled the box of salt out of Crockett's pack, he turned to the men inside the barn. "Y'all ain't gonna eat until after midnight. That lady ain't got a piece of meat in the house. She's gonna have to fry chicken and roast a pig."

"Chickens and pigs! Boy that sounds good." Jim Ewing shouted as Peaceful went through the barn door and ran through the rain toward the cabin.

It was midnight, according to Crockett's silver watch, when they finally sat down at the table. Crockett held up his hands and nodded toward Peaceful, who very slowly and quietly folded his hands under his chin and gave thanks for the food for the use of their bodies. Then the four men nodded thanks to Mrs. Summers and had chicken and corncakes.

"I'm sorry I couldn't make biscuits," Mrs. Summers busied herself filling the cups full of milk as fast as they were emptied by the four men, "but you can't make biscuits without flour."

"The corncakes are just fine, Mrs. Summers." Crockett put two big corncakes on his plate. "We're all from Tennessee, and that means we were all brought up on cornbread. We don't even raise wheat in Tennessee."

"The pig will be ready in a few minutes. It's just not quite done yet. That pig will have to be your dessert. I don't have nothing else to serve. We had dried berries til Christmas, but they're all gone now. If I had any dried berries, I'd make you a berry pie. But they've been gone for two or three weeks now."

"That pig will be just fine, Ma'am." Peaceful licked his lips. "We've been eatin' army rations, just beef and bread, and we've been eatin' it so long, a pig will taste awful good to us."

"We had a calf, but we butchered it as soon as the first cold spell hit, and it's been gone a long time now." Mrs. Summers was turning the pig on a spit in the fireplace.

"This'll be just fine, Ma'am, this'll be just fine." Crockett spoke through a jawfull of fried chicken.

8

After a breakfast of fried eggs and hushpuppies covered with honey had been served to all members of the Tennessee Mounted Volunteers, Crockett assigned three men to stay behind and help Mrs. Summers gather her corn crop and get her hogs back into the pens. He assigned Peaceful, Squire Daymon, and the chicken forager to stay behind. Johnny Hays smiled when Crockett called him the chicken forager.

When Crockett learned that Mr. Summers had gone to San Felipe this past October and had not returned, and that the wagon and team had been held in the Holzclaw Stables in San Felipe since October for storage and keep, Crockett assigned Jim Ewing and Andy Nelson to ride down to San Felipe and sign a government chit and use it to pay the storage charged and bring the wagon and team back to Mrs. Summer's cabin.

Crockett mounted his horse. Then he pointed his finger at the five assigned men. "When you five get your jobs done here, you hurry on down to Washington-on-the-Brazos. I'll wait for you there. I've gotta wait a few days to find out what my real rank is in this here army. I'm either a private or a colonel, but don't know which til Governor Smith confirms my commission. Y'all get on down there as quick as you can, you hear?" Crockett admonished the assigned men. Then he and the other seven Tennessee Volunteers rode off to the southeast, headed for Washington-on-the-Brazos, the capital of Texas.

As Crockett rode away, Squire Daymon turned on Mrs. Summers. "How many acres of corn you got out there, anyway?" He was looking off to the northwest toward a field of corn that lay north of the cabin.

"Well, we had twenty-seven acres of corn, but the deer got some, the coons got some, the cow got some, and the hogs got some. They ain't much corn left. I doubt if there's more than ten or twelve bushels of corn in that whole field."

"Did Mr. Summers gather any corn at all?" Squire Daymon asked.

"No, he left with the cotton before the corn was hard enough to gather."

"What'd'ya think happened to him?" Daymon asked.

"Well, he left here in October with the cotton. I'm sure he was killed, or he would have been back by now, 'cause this is January, and he knows this is the time of year when a woman needs a husband." Mrs. Summers blushed and glanced down at the bulging belly under her skirt.

"When are you expecting, Mrs. Summers?" Squire Daymon asked.

"I'm due in the middle of February."

"How many children you already got, Ma'am?"

"Five." Mrs. Summers put her hand to her mouth and stepped backward a step or two, and then spoke again. "Four. Four's what I meant to say." She raised her apron and covered her face. "I meant to say there would be five after February the fifteenth."

"Yes, Ma'am, you sure need a husband." Squire Daymon glanced at the expectant Mrs. Summers, then at the four children, the largest of which was Little Billy, 10 years old, who had tried to share parental responsibilities by gathering corn and shooting deer and turkey. Billy just wasn't big enough to handle full-grown hogs, and he had let the herd get out of the hog pens and scatter over the hills, living on acorns.

Peaceful and Squire were about a mile from the Summers cabin when they heard a piercing scream. They saw Mrs. Summers screaming and waving her arms. They were on horseback and they had seven grown hogs in front of them and were bringing them in, but they glanced at each other and kicked their horses and rode away from the hogs, racing toward Mrs. Summers and the sound of the scream.

As they rode up, they saw Johnny Hayes holding a half-naked young girl by the arm at the entrance of the chicken house. Johnny turned to them as they rode up. "Look what I found. This pretty little thing was hiding in the chicken house."

Mrs. Summers stormed around the corner of the house with her husband's rifle over her arm she raised the rifle as the hammer cocked back. "You turn loose of my daughter!" she commanded as Peaceful rode up.

"You hid her out from us, didn't you?" Johnny Hays still held on to the girl's hand, admiring her trim slender figure. She held a thin white blouse in her hands, holding it low, like she didn't want it, was about to drop it on the ground. She was looking at Johnny Hays. Her eyes said she liked what she saw.

"Yes, I hid her from the likes of you." Mrs. Summers pointed her rifle.

"You didn't hide her good enough for ole Johnny Hays." Johnny held the hand of the girl and turned her quickly. The girl was between him and Mrs. Summers.

"Hold on now." Squire Daymon climbed off his horse and ran toward Johnny. "We're not gonna have any female trouble." Squire grabbed Johnny by the hand and tried to separate him from the young girl.

I don't like the idea of her hidin' this 'un out." Johnny jerked his head toward Mrs. Summers. "Feedin' us chicken and pork and hidin' out her pretty daughter." Johnny Hays' eyes studied the pretty blonde girl. "She likes me. She put her arms around me the minute I let her outa that chicken house. She took off her blouse; I didn't."

At that instant, Billy Summers came around the east side of the house with his rifle held up, wobbling as usual. Billy reached up and stuck out his tongue and licked his finger then as he pulled the hammer back on his rifle. He shut one eye as he raised it to his shoulder. "You turn loose of my sister!" Little Billy commanded.

Johnny Hays could see Billy had a perfect shot at him. He tightened his grip, ignoring Little Billy. "Aw, I was just lookin' at her." He stared at Billy, then he gave a grudging look to Mrs. Summers. "There's no law against lookin', is there?" He blinked and grinned, shaking his dark handsome head as he admired the young girl's naked round breasts.

"You get on your horse and you get out of here." Billy Summers kept his gun pointed at Johnny Hayes.

"Ellen, did he bother you any?" Mrs. Summers asked.

Ellen studied her mother for a long time and finally turned to Johnny Hays as she shook her head. A tiny disappointed smile creased her lips. She didn't speak or say a word.

"Shall I shoot him, Ma?" Little Billy Summers had his rifle up to his shoulder and one eye shut. He was reaching for the trigger when Mrs. Summers held up her hand.

"Don't shoot him," Mrs. Summers cried out. Billy had his rifle up with one eye shut, and the barrel was wobbling. There was no telling who he might shoot. Mrs. Summers turned and pointed her arm at Johnny Hayes. "Now I'll thank you to turn loose of my daughter."

"She's not complainin'." Johnny Hays held onto Ellen's hand and admired her trim figure and full breasts.

"Ellen can't speak. She hasn't spoken a word since the day she was born." Mrs. Summers advanced toward Johnny Hayes.

"Stay away woman. I've got me a pretty thing, and she likes me and I ain't about to turn loose of her."

"Shall I shoot him, Ma?" Little Billy asked.

"Shoot off his left ear," Mrs. Summers ordered.

41

BLAST! Little Billy's rifle wandered and wobbled, but his aim didn't wander. He took the top right off of Hays' ear. Only it wasn't Johnny's left ear; it was his right ear.

Johnny Hays dropped to the ground like he had been shot through the head. He turned loose of Ellen as he fell to the ground, but Ellen didn't run away. She stood over him for a second, then leaned down and touched his face tenderly where a drop of blood had fallen from his ear. Ellen tore a piece of cloth from her white skirt and began to dab at Hays' bleeding ear. She turned his head around so she could see the little crease cut in the top of his right ear. She bent over very gently and kissed the ear where he had been shot.

Meanwhile, Billy was reloading his rifle as fast as he could, ramming a new charge down the barrel. "Shall I shoot him again, Ma?" Billy asked. He spoke with the ramrod still held between his teeth.

Mrs. Summers shook her head. "No. I think we've had enough shooting for this morning." She leaned over and pulled Ellen up before Ellen got lower, closer, before she could kiss Hays again. Mrs. Summers held her daughter by the hand. Ellen wasn't looking at anybody but Johnny Hays sitting on his butt feeling of the top of his wounded ear. Ellen held out her hand toward him as if she'd like to.

Mrs. Summers jerked her daughter back to her side. "Ellen and I will help fix the pigpen and we'll help you get those hogs in. Then we'll help you gather the corn. I don't think you'd better stay here any longer than you have to." Mrs. Summers turned and looked at her daughter. "Pick up that blouse and put it on." She stomped her foot at Ellen. Then she turned to Peaceful and Squire Daymon. "Ellen is a strange person. She likes men. She takes to men like a duck takes to water. She doesn't know that she isn't supposed to love every man that comes along. And she's so pretty, we have to hide her out when company comes."

42

"Yes, Ma'am, she sure is pretty." Johnny Hays climbed to his feet. She's a mighty pretty girl. She's as pretty a girl as Billy is a good shot." He walked over to his horse.

"I'll take care of Johnny Hays, Mrs. Summers," Squire Daymon spoke. "Don't you worry none about him. Don't you worry no more. He's a Tennessee Volunteer. I'll shoot him if he touches your daughter. An' soon as we get your corn gathered an' your hogs penned we'll be on our way. I promise you nothing will happen to your daughter." Squire Damon pushed Johnny Hays toward his horse. Johnny Hays' lusty Tennessee grin promised nothing. Squire mounted the horse and leaned out his hand and pulled Johnny on the saddle behind him. "Stead o' checkin' hen houses, mebbe you better help me an' Peaceful, we need help herdin' hogs anyways."

As they rode away Johnny Hays turned from his perch behind the saddle and looked back at the cabin. He hugged Squire Damon in front of him, "Boy, she's thu prettiest gal I ever seen. Give me 5 minutes with her an' I'd let that lady shoot me." Johnny slapped his hat against his leg and laughed, "I wouldn't pay no 'tention if she shot me, 'twouldn't hurt a bit."

Squire turned back toward Hays. " 'Twasn't Mrs. Summers who was spoiling fer a shot, 'twas that Billy boy; if he hadn't shut the wrong eye, he'd of blown yer dern head off."

Ellen picked up her white blouse, wrinkled her nose at it with disapproval, and put it on slowly. She didn't button it, but sniffed at it with a rebellious, mischevious, stubborn grin. She walked in the cabin with her breasts still bare under her unbuttoned blouse.

When Johnny Hays and Squire Damon rode up the hill shouting and waving their hats, the hogs took off running, and ran straight to the hog pen. Johnny dove off the rear of Squire Damon's horse and rolled a log to repair the pen while Peaceful shut the gate. One hog broke through the gate just as Peaceful tried to shut it. Squire Damon pulled his rifle out of its scabbard and shot the hog.

43

Squire Damon saw Mrs. Summers running out of the back door waving her arms. Squire Damon bent over then he looked up and apologized, "Thought yu might need a little pork fer supper." Mrs. Summers had both hands on her hips. Squire Damon pointed at the penned hogs, "We couldn't let no hawg set a bad example, Mam."

Squire Damon butchered the hog, turning it into hams, bacons, shoulders, pork chops and sausage, while Peaceful and Johnny Hays gathered the corn.

Everybody ate good that night. Mrs. Summers fed everybody at her table, but when it got dark she led the way to the barn with her tallow lantern and pointed to the hay loft. She pointed her lantern at the sapling ladder, she handed the lantern to Squire Damon, "you take this here lantern to see to keep your men folks in the hay loft."

Squire Damon held the lantern handle in his teeth as he climbed the crude sappling ladder to the hay loft. "Up ye go Johnny Hays," Squire waved the lantern for Johnny Hays to follow him up, and as Johnny got to the top Squire Damon asked, "Do I have to tie ye?"

Johnny Hays shook his head. "I don't have to leave."

"You bother that girl an' I'll . . ."

Johnny Hays laid his rifle down beside his bedroll and looked at Squire Damon with a challenge, "An' ye'll do what?"

"I'll kill yuh." Squire nodded his head, he sat his rifle next to his bedroll. Then he moved his bedroll and his rifle off of the soft hay and right in the path to the ladder. He moved his rifle and sat it next to his bedroll.

Johnny Hays got up and moved Squire Damon's bedroll, he pulled it to the north, out of the path from the hay to the loft ladder.

"Ah can't have you sleepin' on wood, you gotta sleep up here where thu hay's soft." Johnny patted the hay next to Squire Damon's bedroll.

"I'm tellin' you, Johnny, if you..."

44

"I ain't leavin' thu barn." Johnny cut Damon off. He grinned, "I ain't even leavin' this here hay loft."

"You ain't?" Squire asked.

"No, I ain't leavin'." Johnny laid down on his bedroll.

Squire Damon looked at Johnny and then at the path to the loft ladder. "Why did'ja move ma' bedroll?"

Johnny grinned his cocky grin. "Ay, just didn't want her gettin' in your bed 'stead 'o mine."

Squire Damon shook his head and crawled like a big bearded bear into his bedroll. He was soon asleep.

Johnny Hayes blew out the tallow candle and crawled into his bedroll.

Peaceful was nearly asleep when he heard the crack of the leather hinge at the barn door, then he heard light steps and delicate hand holds coming up the hay loft ladder. Peaceful peeked a glance out from under the edge of his blanket. He thought he saw thin white naked feet moving from the loft ladder.

He never saw or heard another thing. He went to sleep, thinking the naked feet was just a dream. All imagination.

Squire Daymon, being the oldest, took charge of the five-man delegation after they left Mrs. Summer's house. They headed southeast till they came to the Brazos River, then followed the river down the east side til they came to the ferry, hallowing and shouting til Bill Munsey poled his ferry across the river and carried them to the west side. Bill Munsey wouldn't let them leave til each one had signed a commissary check for a dollar, the charge for ferrying a horse and man across the wide Brazos River.

There was no town on the west side of the Brazos. They scratched their heads, wondering what happened to Washington-on-the-Brazos, the capital of Texas. They crossed a low, swampy bottom, and then climbed a steep hill. At the top of the hill was a long, sloping plain, a general rise extending westward at least half a mile, spotted here and there with huge shade trees. A tiny sign read, "You are entering Washington-on the-Brazos, the Capital of Texas."

Washington-on-the-Brazos was a town that looked like a camp meeting was about to be held, full of wagons and teams and horses. The provisionary capitol of the State of Texas was located on a hill on a bend of the Brazos River. The stable was the biggest building in town, it being mostly a log barn with a square log-walled lot behind it for holding horses.

John Lott's Hotel was the first building, located on the south side of Main Street. The second building

46

was the Commercial House, where the convention was sitting. The third building was the S.R. Roberts Hotel, followed by the Belew Grocery Store, Post Office, and Barber Shop.

The Lott Hotel was run by Mr. John Moore. The Commercial House, where the Convention delegates sat, was a forty-by-twenty log building with two doors. One of the doors was in the middle of the front, facing Main Street. The other door at the rear had been boarded with logs to prevent anyone from entering or leaving without passing by the doorkeeper, whose main job was to keep drunks from coming into the building. A long, thin, rough-hewn table covered much of the lower floor of the building, running north and south almost half the length of the room.

The chairman, Governor Smith, sat in a huge leather-covered chair at the south end of the table. There were no seats for visitors, just for delegates. The president of the convention of delegates was Richard Ellis, delegate from Red River County. Two delegates, Jesse Grimes and John W. Moore, were arguing with George C. Childress, author of the Texas Declaration of Independence, which was at that time being drawn and prepared by Mr. Childress.

Peaceful returned to Ole Blue and tied him to the hitching rack outside the capitol building.

The wet odor of chewing tobacco mixed with the white fog of pipe and cigar smoke met Peaceful as he climbed the three steps to the door of the capitol building. Peaceful looked inside, leaning around the doorkeeper. Crockett was easy to spot. He was the only man there who wore a coonskin cap. He sat in a cane-bottom chair near the big chair occupied by Governor Smith at the head of the long, narrow, rough-hewn table that filled the center of the lower floor of the big building. Crockett was leaning over telling a joke to Governor Smith, who was laughing and pounding the table. If anybody was tending to business, Peaceful couldn't see it. He counted fourteen men in the room. Each seemed to be doing something different. The only thing they all were doing was either smoking or chewing tobacco. There was a clay spitton beside every chair in the room.

Crockett saw Peaceful take off his black hat and nod his head and wave his hand. He got up slowly, pounding Governor Smith on the shoulder and talking to him. Crockett continued talking to Smith as he walked away, pointing toward Peaceful and Squire Daymon waiting outside the door.

"Well, I see you finally got here. You get that woman's hogs caught and her corn gathered?" Crockett asked.

"Yes, Sir, we sure did," Peaceful answered quickly.

"Yeah, and ole Johnny Hays got the top of his right ear shot off," Squire Daymon laughed and slapped Peaceful on the shoulder. "He found Mrs. Summer's pretty daughter hid out in the chicken house. Ole Johnny didn't quite turn loose of her quick enough, and little Billy shot him through the ear," Squire Daymon laughed.

"Shot him through the ear!" Crockett held up both hands in anguish.

"Yeah," Daymon continued, "did you ever notice how that little boy's barrel wiggles and wobbles when he's aimin' at somethin'?"

Crockett nodded his head.

"Well, Billy asked Mrs. Summers if he could shoot Johnny Hays 'cause ole Johnny was still holdin' on to this pretty Summers girl, and Mrs. Summers said, 'Yeah, shoot his left ear off.' You know what? That boy just fired that gun and shot the top right off Hays' ear. Only it was his right ear." Squire Daymon laughed and banged Peaceful on the shoulder again.

"Did Ewing and Nelson get in with the wagon alright?" Crockett asked.

"Yeah, they had to sign a commissary check for twelve dollars to pay stable charges. While they were signing commissary checks, they just went on down to the grocery store and laid in a supply of sugar, salt, coffee, flour, and molasses. Yeah, and we butchered a

48

hog for Mrs. Summers before we left."

"That's good," Crockett nodded his head.

"Colonel, did you get your rank all worked out?" Peaceful asked.

"Well, let's put it this way: I told ole Governor Smith every joke I know, and I'm still Private Crockett."

"Well we can't have a private in charge of twelve men," Squire Daymon argued.

"Yeah, and we can't have a colonel in charge of twelve men either," Crockett laughed.

"But I heard Governor Smith call you Colonel Crockett when you left the table," Peaceful observed.

"Yeah, the Governor wants me to be appointed Colonel. He appointed me Colonel but the delegates haven't confirmed the appointment you see, these delegates don't seem to want to do anything the Governor wants done. Each one of these elected delegates has some man from his home town that he wants to be appointed captain or major of Colonel or general. They have to vote on every appointment. The only reason Sam Houston got elected General and Commanding Officer was because he was the only governor that showed up," Crockett laughed. "There weren't no other governors, or he might not have been elected. Still, the vote on Commanding General was kinda close. Houston got the most votes, followed by Jim Bowie, then Stephen Austin, and then William Barrett Travis — that's the fellow whose wife you crossed Louisiania with. He got a lot of votes, but not enough to be elected General."

"Aw, but he's just a kid; he ain't but twenty-six years old," Squire Daymon raised his hand, waving away the thought of William Barrett Travis.

"Well, he's a young 'un, alright, but he captured the imagination of everybody with his courage. Seems he captured a cannon from a Mexican captain by the name of Tenorio, and then he just turned the cannon around and dared the captain to come take it away from him. The words he used, COME AND TAKE IT, was on the battle flag the Texas Army used when

49

they ran General Cos, the Mexican General, out of San Antonio last November."

"Colonel, you mean you've been here three days and you ain't got no rank yet?" Squire Daymon asked.

Crockett shook his head. "General Sam Houston said he was gonna try to work out a commission for me as a colonel, but that's all he said." Crockett bit his lower lip. "All I am right now is a member of the Texan Army. Nobody's decided if I got any rank at all." Crockett stared at the tobacco-chewing delegates sitting around the big long table. He grinned. "If I had three months to spend parked around here, I imagine I could work out any commission I wanted. These delegates make me a little sick. They remind me too much of the United States Congress. They spend too much time decidin' who gets the credit instead of gettin' the job done."

"What'cha gonna do, Colonel?" Peaceful asked.

"Let's get the hell outta here. Let's see if there ain't a little more excitement at the Alamo in San Antonio. This place reminds me of a bunch of old women at a quilting bee."

10

Crockett put his hand on Peaceful's shoulder. "Peaceful, will you run over to Lotts Hotel and draw us some provisions? We need salt, beans, coffee, two hams, a side of bacon, and a keg of flour. You sign my name on the chit, then meet us at our camp. You'll find me and the boys camped under an oak on the creek about a mile and a half north of town. It's a pretty place. You'll like it."

"Yes, Sir," Peaceful saluted. "Where are we headed from here, Sir?"

"From here we head for San Antonio."

"They gonna be any Mexican soldiers at San Antonio?" Peaceful asked.

"I understand there won't be any Mexicans there until spring," Crockett answered. He looked at Peaceful for a long silent moment, then he asked, "Peaceful, are you gonna have the same trouble shooting Mexicans that you had wringing chickens' necks at Mrs. Summer's house?"

"I don't think I'll have the same trouble shootin Mexicans that I had when I was asked to wring a chicken's neck at Mrs. Summer's."

"Well, I hope not." Crockett stalked away.

Peaceful rode Ole Blue slowly the twenty yards up Main Street to the Lott Hotel, wondering what he was going to do when he was asked to shoot a Mexican soldier.

He carried his rifle into the Hotel. He remembered what Squire Daymon had said about a man in the army always carrying his weapon with him. He found Mr. Moore reading a newspaper, sitting in a rocking chair at the door to the boardwalk in front of the Hotel which also served as a grocery. Peaceful touched him on the shoulder. "I wanna draw provisions for Davy Crockett's Mounted Volunteers from Tennessee." He glanced around at all the people who were suddenly looking at him.

"Yes, Sir." Mr. Moore rose suddenly. "Miss Price," he nodded at a pretty young thing in shimmering blue standing behind a counter just inside the door of the hotel, which also served as a store, "Will you fix this man up with provisions for Davy Crockett's Mounted Volunteers?"

Peaceful walked into the hotel slowly, looking at the people who were staring at him. He wondered why everybody was looking at him that way. He turned to Miss Price. Her blue eyes were fluttering. She nervously touched her blonde curls and smoothed the white scarf around her neck.

"Mr. Crockett, if you'll tell me what provisions you need, we'll see if we can't fix you up right away."

Peaceful looked at her for an instant and tried to shake his head. "But I'm not . . ." he gulped. He saw everybody in the hotel was watching him. He fumbled and couldn't find the words. "I'm just with the Tennessee Mounted Volunteers, Ma'am. We just need a few provisions." He stopped and scratched his head and rubbed his face, trying to remember what it was Crockett had told him to order. He was looking at a glass case on top of the counter that contained pieces of candy. He wondered if Crockett would mind if he added a bit of candy to the order. "That's the first candy I've seen since I left Tennessee." Peaceful stared at the white pieces of candy in the glass case.

Miss Price pushed back the glass case. "That's some candy I made myself. It's called pecan divinity; it's made out of white sugar and pecans. Try a piece; I think you'll like it." Miss Price reached in the glass case, picked up a square piece of divinity, and handed it to Peaceful.

Peaceful took the candy, but he couldn't look at it. He couldn't look at anything but Miss Price's pretty blue eyes. There was a glow in her eyes that said she thought she was looking at Davy Crockett. She opened her lips a tiny bit, waiting for him to take a bite of her candy, trying to help him. Peaceful took a look at the candy and bit off a piece. It did taste good, delicious. He grinned as he chewed on the candy. "We'll take a five-pound box of salt, a twenty-pound keg of flour, ten pounds of coffee beans, a ham, and a side of bacon." Peaceful licked the tops of his fingers as he ate up the last of the piece of candy. "And oh yeah, a small sack of candy, if you don't mind, Ma'am."

"I'd be delighted." Miss Price began setting pieces of candy on top of the counter. "How many pounds of candy would you like, Mr. Crockett?"

"I've got a sweet tooth," Peaceful apologized. "There's twelve uf us." He scratched his head again. "No, there's thirteen. How about six pounds."

Six pounds coming right up. How long will you be in our pretty little town?" Miss Price asked as she set the salt and sugar and flour on top of the counter.

"I don't know," Peaceful answered, noticing that Miss Price's eyes were fluttering in a way that said she hoped he wouldn't be leaving in a hurry. "We're posted for a fort at San Antonio called the Alamo. Probably be leaving first thing in the morning."

"Oh, I see." Disappointment saddened Miss Price's pretty eyes. "I suppose you're terribly busy. I don't suppose you'll have time to come in for the singing at the church tonight."

"Church singing?" Peaceful asked.

"Yes, we'd love to have you sing with us."

"I'm not much of a singer, Ma'am."

Miss Price nodded her head. "You'll have to come to the smokehouse with me so you can pick out the ham and bacon you want. It's at the rear of the building."

"Just bring me the biggest ones you got," said Peaceful.

"You'll have to come with me to pick out what you want."

53

When Peaceful struggled off the hotel boardwalk to the hitching rack with sacks and boxes and kegs of provisions, Ole Blue gave him a haunted look. Ole Blue seemed to frown, trying to step away and say, "We gotta carry all of that?" When Peaceful got all the provisions tied on his horse, there was no place for him to ride.

"Looks like I'll have to walk," Peaceful laughed.

"We could have tied it on a little better." Miss Price laughed, too. "Don't wear yourself out walking. I want you to come into the singing tonight."

"Aw, I don't know about that." Peaceful smiled and shook his head. "I sing about like a cow that's lost her calf."

"I'll be wearing a blue dress tonight, a blue velvet dress. It's brand new; I've never worn it before. I'd like you to see me in it. I wish you'd come in and stand beside me even if you don't like to sing."

"Well, I'd have to get permission to come in." Peaceful felt Ole Blue nodding him with his head, anxious to get going with his load. He grabbed his horse by the reins before he turned and started walking away. Peaceful wondered why Ole Blue always got in a hurry when he wasn't.

"You have to get permission?" Miss Price asked.

"Yes, I'd have to get permission from Colonel Crockett; he's my commanding officer."

"Oh!" Miss Price had her hand to her lips. "But you signed the commissary ticket. You signed it 'Davy Crockett.'"

"Oh yeah, Colonel Crockett asked me to pick up the provisions and sign his name to the ticket."

"But I thought you were..."

"I'm not Colonel Davy Crockett; I'm just one of his troopers."

"Well, Trooper," the little lady held out her hand, "I'm Alice Price." She shook Peaceful's hand.

"My name is Napoleon B. Mitchell, but everybody calls me Peaceful Mitchell."

"Well, Peaceful Mitchell," Alice clung to Peaceful's hand, "are you coming to our church singing tonight?" she asked, turning her head to one side like she was making an important request.

"I won't know til after I ask Colonel Crockett. I'm in the Army, you know, and I can't go anywhere without asking permission first."

"You be there at seven-thirty. We have church at night in the assembly building. When the delegates to the Assembly are not using it, we have church there."

"I'll try to be there at seven-thirty." Peaceful nodded a salute at her. "I hope you look as pretty tonight in that velvet blue as you do right now." He turned and walked away, leading Ole Blue loaded down with provisions.

11

Peaceful unloaded Ole Blue at the camp north of town under the oak trees. He led him out north of the camp and staked him out where the grass was deep. "Eat fast, ole buddy." Peaceful patted his horse on the shoulder. "We're goin' to church tonight. There may not be any grass around the assembly building."

He looked at the sun still high in the sky as he walked back toward camp, wondering how long it was til 7:30. He walked slowly toward Colonel Crockett, who was leaning against an oak tree with a jug of whiskey between his knees, laughing and joking with Little Joe Bayliss and Johnny Hays.

"I was wondering, Colonel, if I could get permission to go to town tonight."

"What you goin' to town for? You tryin' for a commission too?" Colonel Crockett laughed and raised the whiskey jug up and took a big swig, shaking his head and wiping his mouth as he returned the jug to its place between his legs.

"Naw, Colonel, I'm not goin' to town to try for no commission. I just wanna go to town to go to church."

Little Joe Bayliss and Johnny Hays laughed and pounded the ground with their open palms.

Johnny Hayes pointed his finger at Peaceful. "That Peaceful Mitchell's sure some soldier, ain't he? He likes to go to church, and he can't wring a chicken's neck." He laughed so hard that he shut his eyes, slapping the ground and pounding Little Joe Bayliss on the shoulder.

Colonel Crockett finally stopped laughing and looked up at Peaceful. "Son, have you ever shot that gun you've been carrying around for two weeks?"

Peaceful glanced down at the gun he had cradled in his arms. Then he looked out at Johnny Hays and Little Joe Bayliss, suffering in silence, waiting for them to stop laughing. When they finally stopped laughing and waited for him to answer the Colonel's question, Peaceful spoke. "I shoot my gun when I'm hungry."

Little Joe Bayliss and Johnny Hays laughed again. But Crockett kept a straight face, blinking his eyes thoughtfully. Crockett tossed the cork from the whiskey jug in his hands. "Do you ever hit what you're shootin' at?"

Peaceful raised his rifle slowly, suddenly he was staring at the Colonel and the cork. "Colonel, if you're tired of using that cork for a stopper on your whiskey jug, if you'll throw it up in the air, I'll let you see how I shoot."

Colonel Crockett stopped tossing the cork. He held it between his fingers and looked at it. "What'd'ya think, boys? Are we tired of using this cork for a stopper?"

"It don't matter none, Colonel. He won't hurt that cork none. He couldn't hit if ye held it right at the end of his barrel."

"Well, let's see." Colonel Crockett held the cork in his hand and leaned far to the side. He threw it as high in the air as he could throw it.

Peaceful clicked back the hammer on his rifle and raised it slowly, taking aim at the cork in its slow, lazy arc. He shut one eye and began to squeeze the trigger.

BLAM! The blast jarred Peaceful's shoulders, jerking him backward. For a second he couldn't see through the blue smoke. Then he saw a shower of tiny cork particles floating down from that part of the sky where that cork had been.

"God-damn!" Little Joe Bayliss jumped to his feet and ran out to the spot where the shower of cork particles had fallen to the ground. He picked one up and held it at arm's length, eyeing it and studying it. Then he turned toward Crockett and Johnny Hays. "That Peaceful may not be able to wring a chicken's neck, but he damn sure can shoot."

Peaceful lowered his rifle slowly to the ground and set the butt on the grass beside his foot, leaning on it like a man who had just done something terribly important. He leaned over and blew on the barrel of the rifle and began to reload it. After he had loaded the rifle, he turned to Crockett. "Colonel, am I on Guard Duty tonight, or can I go to church?"

Colonel Crockett looked at Little Joe Bayliss, then glanced at Johnny Hays. He shrugged his shoulders and raised the corkless whiskey jug. "You mighty right you can to to church. I don't want anybody that shoots that straight doing Guard Duty." He laughed and raised the whiskey jug to his lips. He took a big gulp and lowered the big jug with a laugh. "I might come staggerin' in here drunk and I might not know the sentry word." He shook his head again. "I don't want anybody that shoots that straight doing Guard Duty when I'm drinking." He laughed and lowered the whiskey jug between his knees. "You get the hell on to town and leave us old drunk sinners out here to listen to Johnny Hays tell about that little Summers gal with her naked breasts." Colonel Crockett handed the whiskey jug to Johnny Hays. "He's done told me the story twice, and I'm waitin' for him to tell it the third time." Colonel Crockett waved his hand at Peaceful, motioning him away. Crockett laughed again, "Hays says he's in a hurry to get this damn war won so he can head back to that Summers place."

"I don't blame him, Colonel." Little Joe Bayliss grabbed the whiskey jug and put it to his lips, pulling down two big gulps of whiskey. He lowered the jug slowly and wiped his lips. "That little gal had the pr'ttiest breasts you ever saw. Once you see somethin' like that," Little Joe shook his head, "You can get in a hell of a hurry to end a war."

58

"Yeah, just imagine puttin' your nose between those breasts shakin' your head slowly and gently." Johnny Hays shut his eyes. He sighed and shook his head. "The minute this war is over, I'm gonna come callin' on Mrs. Summers, and when I leave there, I'll ride away with that little gal as my bride sure as my name is Johnny Hays."

Peaceful borrowed a bar of soap from Squire Daymon's grub box and walked down the creek to a deep hole of water well below the camp. He undressed slowly, thinking of the bath he was going to take and of scrubbing his hair. He thought of Molly Moffit as he waded out in the creek and got down on his knees and began soaping his hair. "I ain't had a soap bath or hair scrubbin' since Molly cleaned me up and washed my hair so I'd be neat and clean for a camp meeting." Peaceful grinned.

He ducked his head under the water to wash away not just the soap in his hair, but to wash the pain in his chest as he thought of Molly Moffit. The thought was painful and Peaceful didn't like the way it hurt.

Peaceful wondered if that wasn't the way his girl would feel if she knew he was going to the church singing tonight; not to sing, but to be close to Alice Price, to see her in her new blue velvet dress, to hold her hand, look into her blue eyes, and to admire her blonde curls. To squeeze her hand as they stood and sang church songs.

The sun was down and it was dark by the time Peaceful arrived at the assembly building. Wagons and buggies lit with lanterns were arriving as he rode through the town of Washington-on-the-Brazos. He tied his horse at the hitching rack in front of Lotts Hotel. He saw Alice Price standing in the door as he climbed off Ole Blue and wrapped the reins around the hitching rack. He reached up and felt of the bear grease he had used to smooth down his hair as Alice stepped out of the wide door of the Lotts Hotel. She stood on the long porch with her hands behind her hips. She bowed gently and gracefully as Peaceful climbed up the steps and reached his hand out for hers. When she saw his out-stretched hand, she moved back a step.

"Mr. Mitchell, I'm sorry, I forgot to ask you one question."

Peaceful looked at his out-stretched hand and noticed her backward step.

"Yes, Ma'am, we sure didn't talk much, did we?"

"I asked you to come to the church singing with me, but I forgot to ask you one thing." She looked at the ground, then slowly raised her eyes. "I forgot to ask you if you were a married man.

Peaceful shuffled his feet. "No, Ma'am, I ain't a married man."

Alice raised her head slowly, and her eyes brightened. She reached out with both hands. "I didn't think you were, but I've suffered ever since you left, wondering."

Peaceful gave her one hand, but he withheld the other hand. Alice noticed immediately and looked at him.

"I ain't married, Miss Alice." Peaceful looked at Alice's other hand, which was being slowly withdrawn. He looked at her for a long, thoughtful second, wondering if what he was fixing to say was telling a lie. "I ain't married, but I'm spoke for."

Ole Blue snorted and shook his head, wiggling his ears like he had a bad taste in his mouth. Peaceful wondered if Ole Blue thought he was telling a lie. He stared at his horse for a long time. Was he telling a lie? Did Ole Blue think he was telling a lie? Peaceful wondered.

But Alice still had hold of his hand, and she reached out with her other hand and took his other hand in hers.

"But she's in Tennessee, and I'm here." Alice Price laughed.

"Maybe she wouldn't mind me taking you to church," Peaceful volunteered.

"She wouldn't?"

Peaceful shook his head. "She's a trustin' soul." At

the word "soul", Peaceful jerked. "I'm afraid if I go to church I'll..."

"You'll what?" Alice's face lit with a curious smile.

"I might cry."

Alice looked at him with surprise, then she found her voice, "Well, maybe we'd better sit here on the bench in front of the hotel." Alice motioned toward the bench beside the hotel door, a bench covered with buffalo skin.

Peaceful took Alice's hand and led her to the bench and sat beside her. "I'd rather talk than sing," Peaceful grinned. "I ain't very good at either one."

"Well let's just sit here on the bench and talk." Alice smiled at Peaceful. "I'd rather talk to a man than sing, 'specially when it's dark like this." Alice leaned her head against Peaceful's shoulder.

"I wanna ask you a question." Alice squeezed her head against Peaceful's shoulder. "I wanna know what it's like to be a man in the army far away from home." Before Peaceful could speak, she turned to him. "What's it like to be in the army?"

"Now I wouldn't know much about that. I ain't been in the army but 'bout two weeks. I ain't even been shot at, an' I ain't shot anybody. I don't know what kind of soldier I'm gonna make."

"Oh, Peaceful, you'll make a fine soldier. Why, when you came in the hotel this afternoon, you looked so tall and handsome, I thought you were Colonel Crockett."

Peaceful grinned and lowered his eyes bashfully. "But I don't know whether I'm really a soldier or not. Maybe I look like one, but I ain't ever proved I am one. I don't know if I can kill a man."

Alice nodded her head. "You're telling me what it's like to be a soldier."

"Maybe I am." Peaceful felt Alice lean her head against his shoulder. "I guess everybody going to war wonders if they're gonna be a good soldier or not, wonders if they're gonna be a hero or a coward, wonders what it's gonna be like to shoot and be shot at. I know I can shoot. I proved that this afternoon. But I don't know whether I can shoot a man. It's worrying me. It's worrying me like sweatin' out a whippin'. Don't guess I'll know till after it's over, till I see somebody shoot at me."

Alice squeezed Peaceful's hand and stood up. "If somebody shoots at you, you shoot right back." Alice held Peaceful's hands and brought them up under her chin nuzzing them against her neck. "Fact is, Peaceful, don't you wait till they shoot; you shoot first."

"Naw, I reckon I won't shoot first, but if I get shot at, you gotta remember I'm from Tennessee. Volunteers from Tennessee don't shoot first. They shoot last."

"Alright then, you just be sure you shoot last." Alice nodded her head with determination.

"Alright, Alice. I'll try to be there to shoot that last shot."

"What're you gonna do when the war's all over, Peaceful? Are you goin' back to Tennessee?"

"Naw, I ain't goin' back real quick like. First I'm gonna collect my headright, I might get me a ranch and get me some longhorn cows and lasso me some wild mustangs. Someday I might have me a ranch. Then when I get a cabin built and get things fixed just right, then I reckon I'll go back to Tennessee."

"When you go back to Tennessee, will you come through Wasington-on-the-Brazos?"

"Yeah, I reckon I could."

"If you do, I'm gonna try to set a female bear trap an' keep you right here." Alice Price blinked her eyes and nodded her head and squeezed Peaceful's hands.

Peaceful looked to the east, toward the Assembly building. "It looks like ever'body is in church; the wagons 're all empty an' the horses 're hayed."

"Come on." Alice rose and pulled Peaceful off the hotel bench. "Let's go to church. A cry'll be good for you."

Peaceful sat still and quiet, looking at the floor and then at the ceiling. He didn't start crying until the congregation got well into "Rock of Ages" and Alice's soft voice sang:

62

"When my eyes shall close in death,
When I rise to worlds unknown,
And behold thee on thy throne,
Rock of Ages, cleft for me,
Let me hide myself in thee."

Peaceful walked Alice back to the hotel after the services were over. He held her with one hand at the door. "I'm sorry I cried in there," he apologized.

Alice nodded. "The war makes a lot of people cry." She looked out into the street and the lanterned wagons streaming by. "Even some young men."

Peaceful shook his head and drew his hand away. He stared at his hand like he had sinned in touching her. "It ain't the war." He slowly shook his head. "I ain't afraid of dying." He stepped away from Alice, to the edge of the porch, and stared into the night sky. He sighed. "Fact is, I welcome it."

"Oh." Alice raised both hands to her face. "I'm sorry." She clenched her hands. "Oh Peaceful. I'm so sorry." She stepped forward and touched his shoulders with both hands.

Peaceful shrugged her away.

"You've lost a loved one!" she gasped.

Peaceful stared at her, then closed his eyes. His hands rose slowly to cover his eyes. He turned and walked down the hotel steps, mounted Ole Blue, and rode silently out of Washington-on-the-Brazos.

12

They stopped on Powder House Hill almost a mile southeast of San Antonio and only half a mile southeast of the Alamo. The white walled Alamo was on the east side of the San Antonio River, and the city of San Antonio was mostly on the west side of the pretty chalk-colored river with its white limestone banks.

Peaceful saw a rider in white buckskin coming toward them. He rode slowly, and from time to time he looked over his shoulder back toward the Alamo.

The rider rode toward Crockett, and as he reached him, he bent forward in his saddle and turned, shading his eyes, as he looked back at the Alamo. Then he looked at Crockett.

"I don't believe they've hung him yet," he growled.

"Hung who?" Crockett asked, taking a sudden look at the Alamo and the men gathered around a huge pecan tree a few yards to the southeast of the Alamo.

"They're hangin' my friend, Conway." The man in the white buckskin flipped the tips of his bridle reins nervously as his jaw tightened. "Hanging is bad enough, but when it's your friend," he glanced back at the men gathered around the pecan tree, "it's time to ride away. I didn't want to watch his feet kick at the end of a rope, so I thought I'd ride out and meet you." He uncradled his rifle from one arm and stuck out his big right hand. "Jim Bowie's my name."

"Well, I'll be damned." Crockett stuck out his hand and shook hands. "I'm Davy Crockett with a dozen Tennessee Mounted Volunteers." Crockett raised his

64

reins and pushed his horse closer to Bowie and pounded him on the shoulder. "Boys, this here is Jim Bowie, the best knife fighter that ever sharpened a knife in the Southwest."

"I've heard of you, Bowie nodded toward Crockett.

"Nothing good, I hope," Crockett grinned.

Bowie smiled for a thoughtful instant. "Seems to me like I heard after you lost your election to congress that you told President Jackson, 'I'm going to Texas. As far as I'm concerned, you can go to hell.'"

Crockett laughed. "I did say a few words like that." He turned his back to Bowie and looked back at the Alamo. "You say they're having a hanging down there?"

Bowie nodded sadly.

"A friend of yours?"

Bowie nodded again. "Conway was a friend of mine. Fact is, any boy from Arkansas is a friend of mine." Bowie put his hands on his saddlehorn and raised in the saddle, staring down the hill at the men gathered around the pecan tree. "He killed his friend, Sherod Dover. A little dark-eyed dimpled girl messed with 'em both. I never did think soldiers and senoritas mixed very well. She loved 'em both, and now one of 'em's dead and the other one's being hung. I couldn't watch it. I can watch a man die, but not hangin', not over a woman."

"Is that him hanging from that tree there?" Peaceful asked, licking his lips.

"Yeah, that's Conway." Bowie had shaded his eyes, staring at the tree.

"He ain't kicking," Squire Daymon protested.

"You can't see him kicking from up here," Bowie answered. He was watching the men gathered around the tree. Suddenly the men started walking away from the tree. Bowie turned his horse. "Looks like the hanging's over. If you don't mind, I'll ride with you." As they rode toward the Alamo, Bowie shook his head. "Conway and Dover loved the same woman, and now they're both dead. Now that they have nothing to fight over, they'll be buried side by side."

There was something quietly ominous in riding into a fort with a man hanging from a tree with his booted toes pointing upward in stiff agony. Peaceful wasn't the only soldier that gave the hanging soldier a wide-eyed stare.

There were two entrances to the fort, one at the northeast corner and the other at the southeast corner. Men were leaving the hanging and streaming back into the fort through both gates. Crockett chose the north gate. He turned and took another look at the hanging soldier just before he led the Tennessee Mounted Volunteers into the fort.

Inside the gate there was pandemonium; one hundred and fifty men were milling around, half of them in buckskin, a sure indication they were volunteers, and half of them in military greys and greens, a sure sign they were regulars. As Bowie led the Tennessee Mounted Volunteers to the stockade in the northwest area of the fort, Peaceful noticed the men in buckskin all turned and waved or saluted at Bowie. The regular soldiers in military grey or green ignored him.

They had just dismounted when Peaceful heard a familiar voice raised above the din inside the fort. "Sergeant Ward!" the voice shouted. Peaceful turned and saw Colonel William B. Travis on his grey mare saluting a huge bearded heavy-set giant sergeant in stripes, who was not only drunk, having to lean against the walls of the fort for support as he walked, but was also holding a jug cork in his hand and raising the whiskey jug to his lips with both hands as the order from Colonel Travis rang through the fort.

"Yes, Sir." The sergeant stared at his cork for a moment, then stuck it in his jug. He held the jug with his left hand and saluted with his right hand.

"Seargeant Ward, you will take a four-man detail and bury the prisoner!" Colonel Travis shouted his order.

"But now, Sir?" The sergeant, questioned the Commander's order. "But he ain't hung long enough to teach no lesson, Sir."

"Colonel Neil ordered him hung, and I'm ordering him cut down and buried. I want him cut down and buried, and I want it done now."

"Where'll I bury him, Sir?"

"Bury him in the military plot right by the man he killed."

Peaceful wondered if Travis was going to be the commander of the Alamo. He watched Colonel Travis dismount from his horse and walk toward Colonel Bowie, who was about to introduce him to Colonel Crockett. Three colonels in one fort, and only one of them could be Commander.

"Colonel Travis, let me introduce you to Colonel Davy Crockett of the Tennessee Mounted Volunteers." Bowie spoke in a voice that carried both respect and disrespect. Respect for Crockett, disrespect for Travis.

Colonel Travis' jaws tightened when he heard the word "colonel."

"Welcome aboard, Colonel Crockett. I've heard many fine things of you." Travis greeted his fellow officer while they dismounted.

"And I've heard some mighty fine words spoke of Colonel Travis." Crockett dismounted and handed his bridle reins to Peaceful. "I see they're quoting Colonel Travis even on the Texas flag." It was a white flag with a black star, and underneath the star was a black cannon. Underneath the cannon were the words, "COME AND TAKE IT."

"Well, that flag's been here ever since General Cos, the Mexican Commander, surrendered back in November."

"The words 'COME AND TAKE IT! Those are your words, aren't they, Colonel Travis?" Crockett studied the young officer.

"Yeah, I think those are my words. I think I used them after I captured a cannon from a Mexican captain named Tenorio. After I captured it, he ordered me to surrender it to him, and I invited him to come and take it, an invitation he respectfully declined," Travis grinned, "or else I might not be here today." Travis took off his white leather gloves and slapped them against his breeches leg. "Forgive my lack of courtesy! If you will allow me, I will escort you to the officers' quarters. Now that there's three colonels, we'll have to have an election to determine who is the Commanding Officer of this little fort."

"But Colonel Travis, I understood Colonel Neill appointed you Commander when he left." Bowie had one arm around Travis and the other arm around Crockett as he led them toward the officers' quarters.

"He did, but we'll still have to have an election. We can't have three colonels and no Commanding Officer."

"What about James Bonham? Isn't he a Colonel?" Bowie smiled.

"Yeah," Travis returned Bowie's smile, "Bonham makes four colonels, but Jim's an old friend of mine. He wouldn't think of being my commander."

"Four colonels." Crockett laughed. "I'm gonna cut the number down. You can call me Private Crockett when it comes to choosing a commander."

Peaceful noticed that Sergeant Ward, the sergeant Colonel Travis had ordered to bury Conway, picked only Regulars in selecting his burial detail.

"Private Blazeby, Private Cloud, Private Fuentes, and Private Jones. Y'all grab a shovel and follow this jug of whiskey. We're gonna go cut down Private Conway and give him a decent burial."

"Ain't there gonna be no funeral?" Private Cloud asked.

"Murderers don't deserve no funeral," Sergeant Ward growled.

"But every soldier deserves a funeral."

"This one don't."

"Somehow I get a feeling none of us in this fort are gonna get a proper funeral." Private Cloud spoke to the grey-white walls of the Alamo.

13

"Gentlemen, I have assembled you for the purpose of electing the Commanding Officer of the Alamo." Colonel William Barret Travis stood on a wooden cart in the patio of the Alamo. He tried to ignore the rumble of cheers and shouts, the shoving match between the uniformed Regulars and the buckskinned Volunteers. The smiles of the Volunteers were more numerous than the solemn grimmaces of the regular soldiers, but Travis continued. "I contend that I am the highest ranked regular officer in the Alamo and I was appointed to Commander by Colonel Neill before he resigned his command to return to Gonzales to attend to his sick wife. Colonel Bowie and I have a difference of opinion as to whether the appointment by Colonel Neill gives me the right to Command this garrison. We have agreed that each of us will make a little talk and let you vote to select your Commanding Officer." He turned to Jim Bowie. "With your permission, Sir, I will make my talk first and then step down and let you make your talk. Then after we have both spoken, I will go to the east side of the patio and you, Sir, will go to the west side. We will then count the men that follow us, and the Commander will be the one that has the most followers. Is that agreed?"

Bowie folded his arms across his chest. "I don't know that I have anything to say. I am accustomed to letting my gun and my knife do most of my talking. Jim Bowie is a fighter, not a talker. You make your

69

talk, and I will take my position along the west wall. I agree that whoever has the most followers will have won the election and will be the Commanding Officer of this fort."

"Very well, if you do not wish to candidate for the command of this post, then neither will William Barret Travis. Gentlemen, those of you who wish me to be your Commandant will follow me to the east wall, and those who wish Bowie as their Commandant will follow him to the west wall." Before he stepped off the cart, Travis raised his his hands high in the air. "Colonel Bowie says he does his talking with his knife and gun. Let me say Colonel Travis does his talking with a cannon." Travis stepped off the cart, raised his sword into the air, and marched solemnly toward the east wall, eyes forward, glancing neither to the right not to the left as he made his way through the assembled men.

Bowie stood beside the cart until Travis reached the east wall. No men had moved either toward the east wall nor toward the west wall. Bowie glanced around him uncertainly, still not moving. Davy Crockett raised rifle and started toward the west wall, followed by Peaceful and the twelve Tennessee Mounted Volunteers. They reached the shadows of the west wall and turned around. But Jim Bowie still had not moved. He was still waiting at the cart. He slowly moved to the west wall of the patio.

Then the uniformed regulars began milling around, looking at Sergeant Ward, who was leaning on his ramrod, watching the volunteers streaming toward Crockett and the west wall.

Sergeant Ward shouldered the long ramrod. "Don't look at me, dammit!" he cursed. The regulars moved in a circle, staring at Sergeant Ward. He pulled up his breeches with one free hand. "Alright, dammit, if you wanna know who I'm gonna follow, I'll tell you." He marched off toward the east wall. "I'm a regular an' I'm gonna stay a regular. I'm gonna follow Colonel Travis. He's the bastard that started this God-damned war." He marched off to the east wall. All the

70

uniformed regulars followed him.

Travis shook hands with Sergeant Ward as he joined Travis along the east wall. He shook hands and
slapped shoulders with his regulars as he moved
down the line. But he shook hands only with uniformed regulars. None of the home-spun and buckskin-clad
volunteers moved to the east side of the patio. They
moved in a cloud of dust toward Bowie and Crockett
along the west wall.

There was no need to count. Of the 153 men assembled there were 76 regular soldiers along the east wall
and 77 volunteers along the west wall with Bowie.
Bowie won.

Travis walked across the patio with his hand out-
stretched to shake hands with Bowie, but Bowie held
up his hands and shook his head. "I'm afraid, Colonel
Travis, we didn't have an election. We had a division
instead of an election. The regulars want to follow you
and the volunteers want to follow me. That's no way
to command a fort."

"It looks like we can have unity only with joint
Commanders—you in command of the volunteers and
me in command of the regulars."

Bowie nodded.

"Your men will not train," Colonel Travis complained to Bowie.

"Bear hunters are good in a fight, but not worth a
damn at practicing fighting," Bowie grinned from his
seat behind the well near the west wall of the inner
patio.

Peaceful was watching Susannah Dickerson
turning a leg of beef on a spit over the campfire,
watching the meat crackle and pop, turning it slowly,
watching it brown, growing hungrier with every turn
of the spit.

Outside the stone walls of the Alamo, Peaceful
could hear the creak of wooden carts as Mexican families piled their belongings on carts and were slowly
evacuating San Antonio, heading south toward the
Medina River.

"There goes another cart." Bowie studied Travis's

71

solemn face in the firelight. "They've been moving out for two days now. That's a pretty good sign Santa Anna and his army are not too far away."

"I thought Santa Anna wouldn't come until spring, not til there was grass for his horses," Travis smiled. "We did what we could; we burned the grass."

"It's gonna take more'n a grassfire to stop Santa Anna." Bowie glanced around at the men with their rifles cradled in their arms guarding the dark outer walls of the Alamo.

"Yeah, that's why we're here, to stop him." Travis studied the two eight-pounders mounted on a parapet in the inner patio, guarding the south portal to the Alamo.

"You know, it's a funny thing," Bowie observed. "I was sent here by General Sam Houston to destroy the Alamo, and you were sent here by Governor Smith to destroy the Alamo, and we couldn't do it."

"Well, if we don't get some reinforcements, we will be here at the destruction of the Alamo," Travis commented grimly.

"Yeah, maybe we'll get to destroy it after all."

14

"Bowie's drunk." Johnny Hays stood just inside the south portal.

His words brought Squire Daymon to his feet. "What'd'ya mean drunk? We only had the election yesterday electing him Commanding Officer. He couldn't be drunk today."

"Well, he must not of liked winning the election and then having to share the command with Travis, 'cause him and Sergeant Ward are drunker'n a couple of speckled owls." Johnny ambled into the patio with his rifle cradled in his arm.

Peaceful was marching on top of the south wall. He stopped and looked down at Squire Daymon and Johnny Hays, watching the men gather around Johnny.

"Who'd you say was drunk?" Cherokee Campbell joined the throng that was gathering.

"Bowie and Sergeant Ward. They're over in the artillarymen's quarters bending their elbows over a crock of whiskey. Bowie's pounding the table, swearing he was elected Commander. He says he's gonna throw Travis over the north wall."

Crockett joined the gathering as Hays uttered the words. "Wonder why the son-of-a-gun didn't invite me?" Crockett asked with a sly smile.

"I don't think you'd wanna be around him, Colonel. He's stewed. He's pounding that table and kicking chairs. I think he could walk through a stone wall and not even know it was there."

73

"Maybe I'd better go over there and calm him down a little bit," Crockett volunteered.

Johnny Hays shook his head.

"What's he mad about?" Crockett asked.

"He ain't sayin' what he's mad about; he's just bustin' chairs."

Crockett nodded and stared across the patio.

Johnny continued. "He's mad about winnin' the election and then offerin' to share the command with Travis."

"Well that's nothin' to get mad about. He's the one that offered the joint command to Travis." Crockett looked toward the artillarymen's quarters.

"Yeah, but he's mad because Travis accepted the joint command."

"Oh, " Crockett grinned. He heaved a big sigh, cradled his rifle in his arms, and started toward the artillarymen's quarters. "maybe I'd better go over there and empty that whiskey jug before he gets too drunk."

Peaceful looked over the wall to the south and west, and he saw no sign of Mexican troops. He raced down the ladder to join the throng following Crockett to the artillarymen's quarters.

When they reached the artillarymen's quarters, Crockett held up his hand and turned to the men. "I think you better wait here." He started toward the door.

Major Robert Evans, Master of Ordinance, met Crockett at the door of the artillarymen's quarters at the northeast corner of the patio. Major Evans stood in the doorway with his arms folded across his chest. "I don't think you'd better go in there." Evans shook his head. "Bowie's torn the place all to hell. Bowie and Sergeant Ward's gonna have a fight."

"That's why I'm here." Crockett placed his hands on Major Evan's shoulders and set him outside the door. Crockett stalked in the dark doorway.

Peaceful leaned against the door to listen.

"What's the idea of having a party and not invitin' me?" Crockett stumbled to his hands and knees over a broken chair as he stepped inside.

"Get out!" Bowie shouted. "Get the hell outta here!" Bowie wobbled on his feet. "Me and this God-damned Regular are gonna decide who's the better man."

"Aye, leave us be." Sergeant Ward squinted through his drunken Irish eyes. "We're gonna decide who's the toughest, a Regular or a Volunteer. Shut the door and let the best man walk out." Sergeant Ward tossed a bit of chair against the wall.

"My God! Where's Travis?" Major Evans shouted from outside the door.

"Travis has gone to town," Micajah Autry whispered in his Carolina accent.

Crockett pushed the legs of a chair out of the way and closed the door behind him slowly and quietly.

Peaceful glanced over his shoulder at the south wall where he should be marching his post. He shook his head. He knew he couldn't return to that post, not now. He leaned forward, listening, but he heard no fight, no struggle, no noise, only a "splat" like a crock jug breaking on the stone floor.

The door opened sharply, suddenly, and out came Crockett with his arm around Bowie's shoulder. "Out of the way, out of the way." Crockett waved his free arm, pushing men out of his way. "Get out of the Commander's way. Can't you see we're goin' for another jug of whiskey?"

"How'd you stop the fight?" Major Evans asked.

Crockett whispered, "I asked for a drink of whiskey, and then I accidently dropped the whiskey jug. When it busted, I thought they was both gonna whip me." Crockett laughed.

They were half way across the patio when Crockett pointed his arm at Peaceful Mitchell. "Party's over. Everybody back to their posts."

Peaceful raced ahead, with the throng of men following.

Crockett kept one arm around Bowie, steadying him, keeping him on his feet. They crossed the patio and were about to pass through the south portal.

75

A voice called out from the guardhouse immediately west of the south portal. "Hi'ya, Colonel Bowie." Antonio Fuentes places his hands on the bars across the guardhouse door as he shouted at Colonel Bowie.

"Ho, there, Antonio." Bowie and Crockett stopped. Bowie staggered away from Crockett's grip and walked toward the guardhouse door. Bowie placed his hands on the bars of the door and leaned forward, steadying himself. Antonio Fuentes's hands rose and touched Bowie's big gnarled hands. Bowie watched the young man's hands touch his. Then he stepped back. "Antonio, you've been locked up long enough. I'm freeing you."

Juan Sequin stepped out the doorway to the guardhouse. "How's that?" He shaded his eyes from the sun.

"I'm exercising my authority as Commanding Officer. I'm freeing Antonio Fuentes."

"But Sir, he's a thief." Seguin turned and studied the young man staring through the bars.

"Antonio was a thief; he ain't a thief now. Turn him loose."

"But Sir," Juan Seguin rattled the ring of keys in his hand, "you were presiding officer at his trial and his court martial. He can't be freed."

"Unlock the door, or I'll unlock it for you. We need him as a soldier. He can't do no fightin' in the guardhouse."

Seguin stepped backward, holding the keys behind his back.

"Gimme them keys," Bowie stopped Juan Seguine grabbing him by his belt. As Seguin backed up against the wall, Bowie reached around behind him and jerked the keys out of his hand. He felt of the wall, steadying himself as he walked back to the guardhouse door. He tried the third key before he managed to open the door. He swung the door wide. "You are free, Antonio. The Commanding Officer has freed you."

Juan Sequin ran across the patio, past the hospital, the powder magazine, and raced into the courtyard where the horses were stabled. He mounted a saddled horse and rode slowly through the gate into the inner patio and out the south portal. He rode off, toward Colonel Travis, who was grazing his horse between the Alamo and the San Antonio River, watching Mexicans fleeing from San Antonio in the mule drawn carts.

When Travis rode into the Alamo with Juan Seguin, Bowie was asleep. Nobody woke him up. Antonio Fuentes remained free.

15

"Ballentine, this is February 20th. We gotta start looking for Mexicans. I want you and Cloud to maintain a lookout from the tower of San Fernando Church." Colonel Travis pointed to two young men playing mumble-peg witrh their knives in the soft grass near the south portal. "Maintain a twenty-four hour watch, especially to the south and west, and if you see any Mexican soldiers, that's why that bell is in that church tower. Ring it if you see any soldiers coming. We don't want any Mexican cavalry a 'comin' a chargin' in here without warning."

The two young men rose and put their knives away. "Yes, Sir," William Daniel Cloud saluted. "We'll ring the bell and fire a gun, too."

"Just ring the bell," Travis studied the curly-haired young commander. "Don't shoot your gun. We have no amunition to waste." Travis started to leave, but turned for another word. "How old are you, Cloud? You know you have a big responsibility up there."

"I'm twenty-one, Sir. I'll keep a good look-out."

"Where you from?"

"Kentucky, Sir. There's two good watchmen here, one from Alabama and the other from Kentucky, Sir. Johnny Ballentine and me. We'll keep a sharp lookout."

"All right; we will depend on Alabama and Kentucky to tell us when the Mexican Army comes into sight." Travis popped Johnny Ballentine on the butt.

"Shinny up that church tower," he ordered as he walked away.

Colonel Travis paused at the eighteen-pounder at the southwest escarpment. "Sergeant Ward, are you drinking again?"

"Whatd'ya mean 'again'? I ain't never quit," Sergeant Ward grinned. "I don't drink no more'n a half a gallon a day, jest enough to keep my hand steady on this here eighteen-pounder. It's thu biggest cannon in Texas, an' it jest won't shoot straight without a little whiskey to hold her still. Gives a gun jest the right spirit." Billy Ward patted his cannon.

"Don't let me catch you drinking on duty again," Travis warned.

"Don't catch me on duty then," Billy Ward stiffened. "I'm a Regular but also a volunteer, an' if you don't like the way Billy Ward serves as gunner, tell me you don't like my aim and I'll unvolunteer. I'll go home."

"I thought you was from Ireland?" Travis asked.

"That I am, but 'tain't too far to go for a drink."

"Never argue with an Irishman over whiskey," Travis laughed as he walked away. "You take care of your gun, Sergeant Ward; you take care of your gun an' you'll never have trouble with me."

16

"What you doing up so early?" Squire Daymon leaned over the heavy castiron stew pot, adding handfulls of cornmeal to the boiling hunks of beef in the pot.

"I gotta take some groceries up to Ballentine and Cloud. They're keeping a twenty-four hour watch from the bell tower in the San Fernando church. For some reason, they think they gotta eat twice a day."

"Yeah, some people do get some strange habits, such as eatin' twice a day."

"Then Alabama and Kentucky boys have been up in that belfry so long they're about to go nuts. They're beginning to look, talk, and act like a couple of bats. First day or two up there they were grinnin' and braggin' about them pigeon squabs. They made little fires of straw on the stones up there and broiled pigeon squabs. They thought they were in mighty tall cotton. But now they say that just the sight of a bird makes them sick at their stomachs. I think the Colonel ought to change lookouts. I think those boys have been up there too long."

"Well, I'll fill their pail extra full this time; I'll give 'em two pans of cornbread and four pieces of beef." Squire Daymon packed their meals in the pail carefully and handed it to Peaceful.

Peaceful went out the south portal and turned to the southwest, carrying the guards' pail in one hand and his rifle in the other. As he walked around the southwest corner of the Alamo, his head turned north toward the pecan tree a few yards north of the north-west corner of the Alamo. He thought about gathering some pecans and taking them up to Ballentine and Cloud to get their minds off all that squab pigeon they had eaten. Then he thought of Private Conway as he spied the heavy limb where he had hung the morning Peaceful arrived. He decided the two guards wouldn't want any pecans from that pecan tree. He crossed the river and headed west toward the San Fernando church, almost a half a mile away.

Carts were still being loaded and starting their trek to the south and to the southwest. Dark-faced men in their sombreros walked beside their oxen pulling the carts, flipping their whips at the oxen, ignoring Peaceful, having eyes only for their carts and their families huddled on top of the baggage.

Inside the church Peaceful saw several Mexican families kneeling at the altar in humble prayer. Men were in the church this morning, not just women and children, holding candles high in their hands, seeking guidance from above, not knowing whether to stay or leave.

Pigeons flitted from their perches inside the stairway leading to the belfry. Their wings stirred up dust that seemed both nasty and holy.

At the top of the ladder, Peaceful stuck his rifle through the opening, then his bucket of groceries. He climbed into the bell tower slowly and wearily.

"Well, it's about time." William Cloud raised from his blanket in the straw near the window of the tower. "What time is it, Peaceful?" Cloud leaned on his elbow. "We don't know what time it is; we don't even know what day it is."

"Well, it's about 8:00 in the morning," Peaceful smiled as he climbed into the tower and pushed the bucket of food toward Cloud. "And it's the 23rd of February."

"We've been up here nearly three days. We're about to grow wings and fly away." Ballentine turned from his stand at the window. "If them Mexicans don't turn up pretty soon, we're gonna jump from the window."

"I think Colonel Travis has done forgot all about you boys." Peaceful leaned his rifle against the window sill and stared out the window to the west and southwest.

"He'll know we're here if we ring this bell." Ballentine reached over and touched the bell rope.

Peaceful wasn't watching Ballentine. He was leaning out the window squinting his eyes to the southwest. "Hey, I see somethin' out there." Peaceful leaned a little farther out the window. "I see cavalrymen in green and white." He turned and looked at Ballentine and Cloud. "We got any cavalrymen wearing green and white?"

Both men joined Peaceful at the window. They stared at a line of mounted men in the edge of a grove of trees at the top of the hill west of San Antonio.

Peaceful stared at Cloud. "Can that be some of the garrison from Goliad?"

"Look at 'em, Must be a hundred. Mebbe more'n a hundred." Cloud leaned forward, pointing his finger. "Look at them black pompaded caps. We ain't got nobody in a uniform like that." Cloud withdrew his pointed finger slowly. The three men stared at each other with ominous stares.

"They ain't movin'. They're just standin' there, with their horses' heads bowing in the wind. If that was Fannin from Goliad, they wouldn't just be standin' there lookin'. They'd be gallopin'."

"Well, what're we gonna do?" Ballentine asked.

"Ring the bell!" Cloud shouted. "We been waitin' three whole days to ring that bell. Let's ring it." He ran over and began pulling on the rope.

Peaceful placed his hands over his ears to stifle the sound of the bell pealing directly over his head. He stepped backward toward the window, trying to get away from the bell with its sombre saintly thunder. In the city below, Peaceful could see people standing still, turning and staring at the bell tower, pointing, shouting. Some were waving their arms and shouting in glee. Others turned their heads and walked away into the shadows. Off to the east, in the Alamo, Peaceful could see the guards along the walls standing still, staring at the bell tower. Some stood with their rifles cradled in their arms, some stood with their rifles at their sides. There was no shouting or arm-waving in the Alamo, only immobile, awe-struck men.

An officer on a white mount came racing out the south portal of the Alamo and turned west, heading directly toward the San Fernando church. It looked like Colonel Travis hurrying to the church to see what Peaceful, Ballentine and Cloud had seen. Peaceful watched him race his horse and leap off before it came to a stop at the gate to the church. He heard the pigeons in the stairway below fluttering about as Travis raced up the steps.

Off to the west, Peaceful saw the cavalrymen in green and white turn their horses and disappear back into the woods just as Travis stuck his head into the hole in the floor of the bell tower.

"Where are they? Where are those Mexicans?" Travis asked, as he climbed into the bell tower.

"Right there. Right there, Sir." Cloud leaned out the window, pointing his arm toward the cavalrymen disappearing into the woods.

When Travis reached the window, there was not a horseman in sight. He placed his arms on the windowsill and and leaned out the window, staring to the southwest. Then he moved over next to Ballentine and aimed his eyes right down Ballentine's arm toward the grove to the southwest. He shut one eye, staring, following Ballentine's arm. Then Travis raised up and looked at Ballentine.

"Where are they? I don't see any soldiers."

"They're right there, Sir. They just turned around and rode back into the woods." Cloud pointed in the same direction Ballentine was pointing.

There was not a soldier to be seen.

"Who rang that bell?" Travis pointed accusingly at the bell rope.

"I did, Sir." Cloud offered a nervous salute to Colonel Travis.

"Why the hell did you ring it!" Travis shouted. "I told you to ring the bell when you saw Mexican soldiers!"

"But I saw them, Sir; more'n a hundred."

"But I saw 'em too, Sir." Peaceful stepped forward. "They were in green and white with black pompaded hats. It looked like at least a hundred cavalrymen. They didn't look like any soldiers I ever saw before. They just stood there with their horses' heads nodding in the wind. They turned back into the woods when the bell began to ring. That's why they weren't in sight when you got here."

"You saw them?" Colonel Travis pointed his gloved hand at Peaceful.

"Yes, Sir. I saw them. They weren't any of our men. I saw them turn and start riding back into the woods when the bell rang."

Travis returned to the window for another look. "Well, just 'cause I don't see 'em don't mean they're not out there." He turned to Cloud and Ballentine. "Gentlemen, accept my apologies."

Cloud and Ballentine nodded their heads.

"Well, let's get the hell outta here." Travis walked to the ladder. "We've got some gettin' ready to do."

17

Bowie, Crockett, and Travis were standing beside Sergeant Ward's eighteen-pounder at the southwest corner of the Alamo looking west down Soledad Street watching Mexican cavalrymen four abreast ride down the broad avenue.

"What time is it?" Travis turned to Crockett.

Crockett reached inside his buckskin jacket and pulled out his silver watch. He opened the case and stared at it for a second, then shut it and looked at Travis. "It's 2:30 p.m., February 23, 1836."

The cavalrymen turned north at the Military Plaza near the old presidio and formed a military square as more and more cavalrymen marched through the cheering crowds to form their square on the Military Plaza inside the city of San Antonio. After the square was formed, an officer on a white horse bearing a flagstaff with a white flag began riding out of the center of the square, heading east toward the Alamo.

"Maybe they wanna surrender," Crockett grinned.

"They wish to talk." Travis studied the handsome officer in his green jacket, white pants, and black pomadore hat. "Could that be Santa Anna?" Travis asked.

Bowie lowered his head and took a quick look. "Naw, Santa Anna's a heavy-set man of forty. He ain't near that good-looking."

The Mexican officer paused at the San Antonio River and waved his white flag.

"Bowie, you take Sequin and Juan Badillo, and you meet him at the river bridge and see what he wants," Travis said.

"Yes, Sir."

Bowie rounded up a white horse and tied a white handkerchief to the barrel of his rifle, and he and Seguin and Badillo rode out the south portal and turned west toward the San Antonio River. They paused on the west side of the river directly opposite the Mexican officer on the east side of the river.

The Mexican officer lowered his white flag to half staff and offered a smart salute. "I am Colonel Juan Almonte. I am on the staff of General Santa Anna, President of the Republic of Mexico. I have come to discuss the terms of surrender."

Bowie edged his white horse forward, then returned the salute of Colonel Almonte. "You speak excellent English, Colonel Almonte. I did not expect to hear English from a colonel on the staff of General Santa Anna."

"I am fluent in four languages and a graduate from one of your better schools in Massachusetts. Whom do I have the honor of addressing, Sir?" Colonel Almonte saluted polietely.

"I'm Colonel James Bowie. I'm not accustomed to talking under a white flag. I understand you have to come to discuss terms of surrender."

"James Bowie!" Colonel Almonte's horse shifted under him. "I have heard of James Bowie. I expect every person in Mexico has heard of James Bowie."

"What are your terms of surrender, Sir?" asked Bowie.

"Our terms are unconditional surrender. We ask that you lay down your arms and march out peacefully. There is a chance that some of you may be spared."

"We wouldn't be here, Colonel Almonte, if we expected mercy from Santa Anna."

"You are refusing the terms of unconditional surrender?" Colonel Almonte asked.

"We came to fight, Sir, not to surrender." Bowie gave Colonel Almonte a courteous salute and turned his horse and rode away.

Peaceful was marching his round at the west wall when Bowie climbed the parapet to the eighteen-pounder at the southwest corner of the Alamo to report to Travis on the flag of truce.

"Well, Bowie, did you meet General Santa Anna?" Travis asked curtly.

"Naw, that was Colonel Juan Almonte. He spoke better English than I do. Said he'd been to some school in the East."

"Well, what were his terms? What did he offer?"

"Unconditional surrender. He said if we lay down our arms and march out, he might spare some of us."

"The arrogant bastard," Travis cursed. Travis stomped up the parapet and laid his hand on the eighteen-pounder. He turned to Bowie. "Did you tell him I would give him my reply within the hour?"

"No, Sir. I gave him your reply then and there."

"You did?" Travis stood stock-still, staring at Bowie. "But you had no right." Travis placed his hand on the hilt of his sword. "We are joint Commanders. You have embarrassed me; you have humiliated me."

"I told him we came to fight, not to surrender." Bowie was stiff and erect.

Bowie and Travis stared at each other in stiff confrontment. Then a smile cracked on Travis's lips. His face broke into a grin. "Good for you. You said it better than I could." Travis stepped forward and shook hands with Bowie. He placed both arms around Bowie and hugged him to his chest. Then he stepped back and slapped Bowie on the shoulder. "Let's get this fort ship-shape and show them Mexicans how to fight." Travis turned to Sergeant Ward. "Sergeant Ward, load and fire your eighteen-pounder. Let's give them a taste of grape and buckshot."

"Yes, Sir." Sergeant Ward set down his jug of whiskey. He licked his lips and rammed in powder, buckshot, and grape. He patted the rusty old cannon. He sighted down the barrel and raised his match fuse high and shouted, "Ready on the right? Ready on the left?"

Peaceful put his hands over his ears as the match fuse lowered slowly to the match hole of the eighteen-pounder.

The cannon roared and belched smoke. The cannon barrel buckeled backward sharply in the blast.

Across the river, the Mexican soldiers in their green and white with their black hats stopped in their tracks and ducked for cover as the cannon roared. Peaceful laughed and clapped his hands, as did Travis, Crockett, and Bowie. They grinned as they watched the Mexican soldiers dive for cover.

One Mexican soldier didn't dive and run. He hoisted his rifle across his chest and marched slowly toward the river.

"Can I have him, Colonel?" Crockett grinned at Colonel Travis. Travis nodded his head.

Crockett raised Old Betsy slowly to his shoulder and took slow steady aim. When he fired, he didn't move. His aim was still on the man on the west side of the San Antonio River.

The black-hatted man in green and white stood for a haughty instant. Then his rifle flew into the air and his arms rose into the sky as he tumbled backward. His hands grabbed at his head and his feet kicked a couple of times, and then he lay perfectly still.

"You can bet your boots on one thing. That ain't the last one." Crockett lowered his gun slowly.

"Good shot, Colonel, good shot," Travis commended Crockett.

"We showed 'em a thing or two about fightin', didn't we Sir?" Johnny Hayes patted Crockett on the shoulder.

"Yeah," Crockett answered. "I reckon we got off to a right good start."

"Sir," Lieutenant Almeron Dickerson saluted Colonel Travis, "three men ran from the Alamo when they saw Santa Anna's cavalry parading down Solidad Street."

"You say three men ran?" Travis asked.

Dickerson nodded his head.

"Who were they?"

"Well, the first one was ole bald-headed Nat Lewis, the grocer. I shouted at him when he started to run, and he turned and shouted back, 'I'm not fighting; I'm a businessman.' He ran like a rabbit trying to hide from a coyote."

"Who were the other two?"

"Captain Dimmit and Lieutenant Nobles. They didn't run like Nat Lewis. They just walked out like they knew where they were going."

"Perhaps they had business to tend to. Maybe they'll be back."

"Well, I couldn't help but notice that when everybody else was rushing to get in the Alamo, these three men were the only ones that were rushing to get out."

"Thank you, Lieutenant Dickerson. I appreciate your report. I am sure Nat Lewis has returned to his store. As for Captain Dimmit and Lieutenant Nobles, I'm sure they will either return or aquit themselves in an honorable fashion. You may return to your twelve-pounder." Travis tossed his quill on his desk and rose to his feet. "Oh, and Lieutenant Dickerson, we're short of ordinance for our cannons. I want you to assign three men to breaking horse shoes into pieces for cannot shot. We will not take shoes from the horses, at least not now." Travis managed a feeble smile. "We won't be needing cavalry, not with the job that's before us. Our need for horses and cavalry is over. What we need now is powder and cannon shells. "You might assign two men to breaking all our stored horse shoes into small pieces for grape shot."

"Yes, Sir." Lieutenant Dickerson saluted as he left Colonel Travis's office.

18

It was night and Peaceful was making his rounds, walking behind the escarpment along the northern wall between the artillerymen's quarters and the officers' quarters. When he got to the northwestern corner, he made a sharp about-face. He paused to look at the huge pecan tree before he made his march toward the east along the wall. He always thought of Conway, who had been hung to a sturdy branch on the east side of that pecan tree the day Peaceful had arrived. He wondered what it was like to die. He thought of two people when he thought of death—Molly Moffit, who used to sit on her swing on her front porch waiting for him, and he thought of his mother in the kitchen baking cornbread, smiling when he dug into the cornbread and spread butter on it, and the way she would come to his bedroom after he had gone to bed, holding her lantern high, watching to see that he had gone to bed.

His mother would cling to her Bible, holding it tightly, knowing that in the Lord's good time, she would be with her son again. But Molly for Molly his death would be...He wondered how she would feel when he died. Would his death give sorrow or comfort? He wondered as he turned at the northeast corner of his post.

Peaceful heard someone shouting from the riverbanks from outside the Alamo. He couldn't understand all the words; they were in Spanish. Then he saw Gregorio Esparza inside the Alamo, racing up the ladder to the escarpment. Gregorio cupped his hands and shouted back in Spanish.

"Who you shouting at?" Peaceful asked.

"My brother," Gregorio grinned sheepishly.

"You got a brother out there?" Peaceful asked.

"Si. My brother Enrique Esparza, he is out there." Gregorio nodded his head toward the river.

Peaceful turned and stared toward the river. "I don't see anybody out there but Mexican soldiers."

"My brother Sergeant Enrique Esparza, he is with the San Luis Batallion of Volunteers under Colonel Morelos."

"You mean you got a brother out there that's gonna be fightin' against us?"

Gregorio nodded his head.

"But why...why would you be fighting in here and your brother fighting out there?"

"Enrique thinks it is better to have a Mexican dictator who speaks Spanish than to have an American president who speaks a foreign tongue."

"What do you talk about?" Peaceful asked.

"Oh, he asks me about my wife and my four children, and I ask him about his wife and his three children." Gregorio laughed. "I am the older brother; I got started before he did."

"What does he say is gonna happen here?" Peaceful asked.

Gregorio sighed. "Enrique say we all are going to die."

"Even you, his brother?"

"The blood-red flag of no surrender is flying from the tower of the San Fernando Cathedral, the highest building in San Antonio. That means there will be no prisoners."

"But you didn't have to stay. You were given the opportunity to leave. You could have climbed the wall and escaped."

"Si. " Gregorio spat, and then he smiled. "I chose my side. The dice has rolled. I must take the conse-

91

quences. Que sera sera."

"Que sera sera?" Peaceful wrinkled his brow. "What in the world does that mean?"

"What will be will be."

"If my brother were out there, I would hate to be in here."

"Si. He should be in here with me."

Peaceful grinned at Gregorio, made a sharp about-face, and marched back down the wall.

19

Peaceful noticed Jim Bonham saddling his horse in the horse corral. Peaceful took his rifle and ambled over in that direction, wondering what a man in the Alamo would be doing saddling a horse after the arrival of Santa Anna's troups. Was he going home? Was there a way to escape from the Alamo? How would he get through the Mexican lines?

Peaceful walked over and began patting the rump of Jim Bonham's fine chestnut mare. "You going home?" he asked Bonham.

Bonham had the stirrups raised and was tightening the cinch strap. He shook his head.

"You gonna try to leave the Alamo on horseback?"

Bonham nodded his head. He led his horse by the reins over to the water well, drew a bucket of water, and poured it into the clay horse trough. He stepped back and walked around his horse, surveying its condition, raising each foot and examining the horse shoe.

John W. Smith came out of the horse corral with his horse saddled. He drew a bucket of water from the well and watered his horse.

The appearance of saddled horses inside the patio drew a lot of attention. Peaceful soon had a lot of company standing around eyeing the two saddled horses.

Then Juan Sequin came out of the horse corral leading Jim Bowie's black mare.

Sergeant William Daniel Ward began climbing off the revetment at the southwest corner of the Alamo.

Peaceful heard him curse as he walked toward the three horses being watered at the water well.

"What's that damn Mexican doing with Jim Bowie's horse?" Sergeant Ward pushed up the sleeves of his powder-burned buckskin jacket as he approached the three saddled horses. He laid one big powder-burned hand on Juan Sequin's shoulder and turned him around with a harsh jerk. "What the hell you doin'?" he demanded as he jerked the bridle reins from Juan Seguin's hand. "What you doin' with Bowie's horse?"

Juan Seguin looked at the powder-blackened hand on his shoulder until Sergeant Ward removed it. Then Seguin held out his hand for the bridle reins.

Sergeant Ward shook his head. "Me and Jim Bowie may have a fight, but there ain't no Mexican gonna ride out of here on his horse. 'Specially not without Bowie's permission."

Juan Seguin took his handkerchief and brushed some dust and powder off his shoulder. Then he turned to Sergeant Ward. "I have Colonel Bowie's permission to borrow his horse." Juan Seguin spoke slowly and confidently with a voice of authority. "Colonel Travis has asked me to go out among my fellow countrymen and raise a Mexican contingent to come to the rescue of the Alamo."

Sergeant Ward frowned and shook his head in disapproval.

"When I fled to the Alamo with you Americans, I neglected to bring any of my horses with me, and I had to borrow from Colonel Bowie his horse. He said he didn't think he would be riding it." Juan Sequin smiled. "Colonel Bowie told me that if he needed his horse, he'd come and get it."

Sergeant Ward still looked at Juan Seguin with disapproval. When Juan Seguin held out his hand for the bridle reins, Sergeant Ward stared at the gloved hand for an instant. He finally placed the bridle reins in Seguin's hand.

Juan Seguin nodded his thanks. "On my ranch south of San Antonio, there are many horses. If

Colonel Bowie ever needs a horse, there will always be a replacement for him at the ranch of Juan Seguin." He put on his black Mexican sombrero, mounted Jim Bowie's horse, and rode to the north gate. He waved to the man who opened the wide wooden door. He rode out in a slow, confident canter.

"I don't trust that feller." Sergeant Ward pointed at Seguin as he rode out the north portal. "He's just ridin' out of here to tell Santa Anna how many men we've got, where our cannons are located, and how much ammunition we've got. He ain't goin' after no help; not for us he ain't."

Peaceful saw Colonel Travis walking up just as Sergeant Ward spoke.

Colonel Travis stepped in front of Sergeant Ward with his arms folded across his chest. "Sergeant, you sound awfully sober this morning." Colonel Travis looked at the huge bearded, tobacco-chewing, whiskey-drinking cannoneer.

Sergeant Ward grinned. "Yeah, I am sober, Colonel, and I forgot to tell that Mexican to bring me a keg of whiskey when he comes back in here with them Mexican Nationals to help us defend this here Alamo." Sergeant Ward pointed toward the north portal with an ironic smile on his face.

"Juan Seguin is a loyal Texas soldier. He will bring re-inforcements if he has time." Colonel Travis turned and placed his arm on John W. Smith's shoulder. "John, I want you to go to Gonzales. Tell them to raise a relief column and send all the able-bodied men they can spare. You'll probably have to bring them in under cover of night, but you know our coyote call. You signal us when you're comin' in, and I'll see that nobody shoots at you." Colonel Travis smiled and shook hands with John W. Smith.

Then Travis turned to Jim Bonham. "Well Jim, I hate to ask a fellow South Carolinan to be a messenger at a time like this, but somebody has to go to Colonel Fannin at Goliad and tell him to fetch his five hundred men up here and help us hold this Alamo." Colonel Travis reached inside his tunic and pulled out a folded letter. "I want you to give him this written request to come to the Alamo. You'll probably have to put the squeeze on him, Jim, because if I know Colonel Fannin, he won't want to turn a finger until he gets General Houston's permission. That's the way them West Point officers conduct their wars. But don't you let him set there. You set your spurs deep and get him on his way up here. 'Cause if he don't get here in a hurry, we won't be here to greet him.'"

Jim Bonham placed both hands on his saddlehorn and vaulted into the saddle. He turned and smiled at his fellow South Carolinan. "I'll ride as fast as this horse can fly. And I'll bring Fannin back with me, provided I can talk that West Point lingo. You know how those West Pointers are. They want orders before they do anything."

"I'm sending him my orders for him to come to the relief of the Alamo." Colonel Travis pointed at the letter in Jim Bonham's coat pocket.

"I'll bring him if I can. I'll set my spurs and see if I can get him moving in this direction." Jim Bonham waved his hat and galloped through the north portal, followed by John W. Smith.

"Reckon any of them will come back?" Johnny Hays asked Peaceful as they walked back toward the north wall.

"Sergeant Ward doesn't think Seguin will come back, does he?" Peaceful frowned as he thought of Sergeant Ward's harsh stare at Juan Seguin. "He's got a hard row to hoe, trying to talk Mexicans into fighting Mexicans." Peaceful smiled and shook his head.

"I don't think any of 'em will come back." Johnny Hays sat down at the fire and folded his arms across his chest, shivering at the cold. "I wish Sergeant Ward had told Seguin to bring a keg of whiskey. It's powerful cold. We could use a little whiskey to warm our bellies."

Squire Daymon raised his head and looked at Johnny Hayes thoughtfully. "Yeah, and there's a few of us that need it for courage."

20

Santa Anna was riding his white horse on the west side of the San Antonio River, riding from revetment to revetment waving his sword, giving instructions, directing his artillarymen. Cannons suddenly came out of their protective revetments and were wheeled to the north, away from the fire of Sergeant Ward's eighteen-pounder in its position at the top of the wall at the southwest corner of the Alamo patio.

"Where the hell are they goin' with them cannons?" Sergeant Ward stepped from behind the eighteen-pounder and shaded his eyes from the sun as he watched the Mexican cannons being wheeled north-westward, away from the range of his eighteen-pounder. "Keep shooting." Sergeant Ward handed his fuse match to John McGregor and pointed to the farther most cannon moving to the north. "Keep shooting, and shoot fast, before they get away."

Sergeant Ward ran along the wall toward Colonel Travis who was watching the shifting of the cannons at his post at the top of the chapel. "Colonel, they're moving those twelve-pounders out of range of my eighteen-pounder. They're headed toward the north wall. You're gonna have to get a twelve-pounder up there, or they'll tear us to shreds."

"We've got an eight-pounder at the northwest corner," Colonel Travis waved away Sergeant Ward's alarm.

Sergeant Ward turned and walked back toward his cannon. He was talking to himself or to his eighteen-

97

pounder. "An eight-pounder can't keep them twelve-pounders back there where they belong." Sergeant Ward leaned over and patted his cannon. "If that roof along that north wall was strong enough, we'd move you over there and put them in their place, wouldn't we gal?" He patted his long-barrelled cannon.

"They're out of range, Sir." McGregor told the sergeant. "They've moved behind those houses along the north side."

"Yeah, I know," Sergeant Ward grumbled. He leaned against his cannon and watched Colonel Travis come tearing out of his post at the top of the chapel. He ran through the chapel and out into the inner patio. He grabbed Lieutenant Almeron Dickerson by the shoulders and turned him around. "We've gotta put a twelve-pounder on top of that north wall."

Lieutenant Dickerson shook his head. "That roof won't hold a twelve-pounder, Sir. It'll barely support a man with a gun in his arms."

Colonel Bowie walked up wiping a cloud of black smoke away from his face. "We've stopped receiving fire on the south wall. What's goin' on out there?" Bowie asked.

"Santa Anna's wheeled his twelve-pounders out of range of Sergeant Ward's eighteen-pounder. He's placed those twelve-pounders behind a row of houses. You can't even see 'em from our eighteen-pounder."

"Major Evans has got two twelve-pounders at the south portal." Bowie pointed to the south portal. "Why don't we put a couple of them on top of the north wall?" Bowie suggested.

"Lieutenant Dickerson says that roof on that north wall won't hold a twelve-pounder," Travis said.

"It's just a shed room, roofed with cottonwood logs. It won't hold up any cannon, let alone a twelve-pounder." Lieutenant Dickerson shook his head.

"Well, we can't stand here and let 'em tear that north wall to hell." Bowie ducked, shading his eyes from a shower of dust from an incoming cannon shell.

Bowie, Travis and Dickerson stood in the patio, studying the thick white cottonwood logs that jutted out into the inner patio from the roof of the shed inside the north wall.

"Those cottonwood logs is where this place got its name. Alamo. The Spanish word Alamo means white wood, or cottonwood logs," Travis informed Bowie and Dickerson.

"Powerful strange that a fort would get its name from rotten old logs that can't be properly defended," Bowie commented glumly.

"We gotta get a twelve-pounder up there." Travis folded his arms across his chest.

"If you want a twelve-pounder up there, I'll put a twelve-pounder up there." Bowie grinned real big. He stepped between Travis and Dickerson to prevent Dickerson from making another protest.

"Thank you, Colonel Bowie. I'd appreciate it very much if you could get a twelve-pounder up there and put it to work."

"I'll need a chain, a heavy ladder, and some support logs." Bowie studied the high roof of the shed room along the north wall, looking at the thick white cottonwood logs that jutted out into the patio. He turned to Lieutenant Dickerson. "If you and your men move that twelve-pounder from the south portal, I'll put it on the roof at the north wall."

"Cottonwood logs were never designed to hold cannons." Dickerson shook his head.

"You get the cannon, and I'll put it on the roof," Bowie instructed. Then he turned to Peaceful. "Peaceful, you and Squire Daymon run over to the supply room and bring me two long sturdy ladders and two chains." Then Bowie turned to Cherokee Campbell and Johnny Hayes. "You two bring four logs. We're gonna need something to support those two ladders while we pull that cannon up. Now hop to it."

Peaceful held one of the longer logs in place under his ladder to support it while the twelve-pounder was being drug up the ladder.

"Heave ho! Heave ho!" Peaceful heard Bowie shout from the roof of the shed room as the chain rattled and the cannon began its slow, bumpy climb up the ladder. The heavy wooden-wheeled cannon creaked and groaned its way up the trembling ladder.

Peaceful felt the log stiffen as the weight of the cannon reached his log's position under the ladder. Peaceful glanced up and caught a thin stream of dust as the yellowed wooden cannon-wheel creaked slowly over the part of the ladder supported by the log Peaceful was holding in place.

"There now! Hold 'er steady!" Peaceful heard Bowie shout.

The ladder was suddenly still. Peaceful's log was no longer stiff with weight.

"We made it!" Bowie shouted with pride in his voice.

Peaceful stepped out from under the ladder and inched back into the patio for a better look. The cannon was on the roof. Cherokee Campbell and Johnny Hays and William Cloud were helping Bowie roll the cannon wheels over a ridged cottonwood log.

"Hold it!" Bowie shouted. "There's a rotten log."

Peaceful heard the crackle of splitting wood. One wheel of the cannon sank through the roof and the other wheel rose into the air.

"Oh my God!" Cloud screamed through a cloud of white dust.

"What happened?" Peaceful shouted and raced up the ladder.

"A cannon wheel fell through the roof." William Cloud eyed the cannon wheel turning in the air above his head. Then he pointed at Jim Bowie smashed into the roof by the wheel that had caved through the roof.

Peaceful ran toward the wheel that had penned Bowie against the cottonwood logs.

"That log's rotten! Watch out!" Squire Daymon shouted as Peaceful took hold of the sunken wheel.

"That log's rotten! Watch out!" Squire Daymon shouted as Peaceful took hold of the sunken wheel.

A log under Cherokee Campbell crumbled, and he fell through the roof into the shed room below. The log on Peaceful's side of the wheel didn't cave in. Peaceful grabbed the wooden spokes of the wheel and heaved with all his might, gritting his teeth, shutting his eyes as he strained and heaved to lift the wheel off of Bowie's chest.

"I got it!" Peaceful shouted through gritted teeth as he felt the wheel raise and crack, then raise a bit more, then a full inch. "Somebody pull him out while I got this wheel up. Pull him out quick."

The rotten log had caved in under Squire Daymon, but he didn't fall through. He slid to his knees to spread his weight over the rotten logs. He reached for Bowie's boots and began to tug him gently. He pulled and tugged till he had pulled Bowie's long frame out from under the sunken cannon wheel.

"I can't breathe. I can't breathe." Bowie ran his fingers lightly over the wheel spoke marks across his white buckskin jacket.

Johnny Hays cupped both hands around his mouth and shouted, "Somebody get a doctor! Colonel Bowie's been crushed by a cannon! He says he can't breathe! Hurry!"

Peaceful let the cannon wheel down slowly and let it reach firm bottom. He turned loose and stared at his hands for a second, gratefully, wondering where he had got the strength to lift one side of the twelve-hundred-pound cannon. Peaceful raised slowly and put his hands behind his back, rubbing and straightening the weary muscles. Then he took two steps toward Bowie and stopped.

Bowie was shaking his head. Sweat was popping out on his forehead. He was clenching his jaws, gritting his teeth. He shut his eyes. One of his hands ran lightly over his crushed chest. The other hand was clutching and clenching the air.

Dr. Amos Pollard climbed up the ladder slowly carrying the handle of his black bag in his teeth. He set the black bag down without ever touching it with his hands. He opened Bowie's jacket, then slowly opened his shirt.

The wheel rim marks and the spoke marks were still

visible on Bowie's crushed chest. Dr. Pollard ran his fingers lightly down Bowie's chest and watched his head jerk back in agony with every touch.

Dr. Pollard had opened his black bag, but now he closed it. He rose slowly to his feet, shaking his head. "Somebody run to the hospital and get a blanket and stretcher. He's hurt bad, and there's nothing a doctor can do."

Johnny Hays took off down the ladder like a jack-rabbit running downhill.

"Is he hurt bad, Doc?" Lieutenant Dickerson asked.

"He's got a double fracture of every rib on the left side of his chest. Everytime he breathes, it hurts every bone in his chest."

"Here comes Johnny with that stretcher and blanket." Squire Daymon met Johnny at the head of the ladder and reached for the stretcher.

Jim Bowie raised his head. "I ain't leaving this roof til that cannon gets pulled out of that hole and put in position and put to work."

"Don't move, Colonel. You're hurt bad. You're hurt mighty bad." Dr. Pollard leaned over Bowie.

Bowie pushed the doctor away with his one good arm. "I came up here to get that cannon to shootin', and I ain't leavin' till it starts shootin', so y'all get it out of that hole and put it to work."

Dickerson shook his head, then grinned. He helped pull the cannon out of the hole in the roof and put it in position.

Peaceful and Johnny were carrying the stretcher across the roof and down the ladder when the twelve-pounder fired its first shot from the roof of the shed room after it had been put in position.

Bowie's pained face cracked a grim, but satisfied smile as he was carried across the patio to his room. He raised up on his stretcher to watch his men defend the Alamo.

That night Bowie resigned his commission as Joint Commander of the Alamo and gave sole command to Colonel William Barret Travis.

21

"Are you a doctor?" Peaceful asked William D. Sutherland.

"That I am, Lad, the best doctor that ever got run out of Alabama."

"Are you a horse doctor?" Peaceful asked.

"Well mostly a man doctor, although I have treated women," Dr. Sutherland laughed.

"Well, my horse, Ole Blue, has got a wooden splinter in his foreleg, and he's neighing and nickering and stomping his foot something awful. I think he needs a little medical attention. I can't sleep as long as he nickers and suffers."

"You mean the Alamo finally sufferred a casualty as a result of all that cannoneering?" Dr. Sutherland grabbed his little black bag and rose from the campfire.

"Yeah, one of those last shells they fired hit a cart in the horse corral just north of the chapel, and a splinter flew from that cart and crippled Ole Blue. He's sufferin' somethin' awful. I can't stand to listen to him nicker."

Dr. Sutherland was going through the east gate to the inner patio. He turned to the left and went through the hospital, then turned to the right into the horse corral.

"If he's hurt too bad, we may have to shoot him." Dr. Sutherland continued walking, but Peaceful stopped short. Then Dr. Sutherland stopped. "What's the matter, Son, ain't you ever seen a horse shot?"

103

"Not my horse." Peaceful held his hand out toward Dr. Sutherland. "You ain't gonna shoot Ole Blue no matter how bad he's hurt."

Dr. Sutherland walked back toward Peaceful. "Touchey about your horse, ain't you Son?"

"Ole Blue is part of my family, just like a brother to me. I hurt when he hurts."

"Well, we won't shoot him. You get a candle so we can cauterize when we get that splinter out."

Dr. Sutherland was standing near Ole Blue leaning over studying the jagged splinter in the horse's foreleg when Peaceful walked up with a lantern and a candle.

Ole Blue was nickering and pawing the ground with his left foot. He turned away from Dr. Sutherland every time he approached. "Don't believe your horse is gonna let me doctor him." He set his black bag on the ground. "He must be a one-man horse."

"He shore is, Doctor. He don't like nobody but me."

"Well, you'll have to get that splinter out yourself."

"I done tried, Doctor. I can't get it out."

"Here, you take these forceps. You walk up there and put your arm around that horse, and you pet him and talk to him and cuddle him. You take the forceps and clamp it on that splinter and jerk it as hard as you can."

Peaceful approached Ole Blue with the forcepts held behind his back. Ole Blue lowered his head and pulled his ears back and studied Peaceful, wondering why he had one arm behind his back. He flipped his ears in the candlelight, but he let Peaceful put his arm around his neck and pet him.

Peaceful began talking to Ole Blue, petting him, rubbing his skin. "Them Mexicans lobbed cannon shells in here all day, and they couldn't hit nothin' but a mangey ole cart, and you had to be standin' next to it. Now you settle down, 'cause we gotta get that big splinter out."

Ole Blue nodded his head as if he knew and understood what Peaceful had said. Then he cut his head to the side as Peaceful brought the forceps out from behind his back and moved them toward Ole Blue's foreleg. Ole Blue began to tremble. He nudged Peaceful on the shoulder with his nose, saying, "Let's get it over with."

Peaceful kept one arm around Ole Blue's neck and ran his other hand down his neck, letting the forceps touch his skin. Peaceful turned to Dr. Sutherland. "Can you get a little closer with that light?" Dr. Sutherland stepped forward with the light.

Ole Blue raised his head in alarm.

"There, that's good, I can see." Peaceful hugged Ole Blue as tightly as he could and opened the forceps as wide as it would go. He slowly moved it toward the splinter, opening it over the splinter until the forceps nearly touched Ole Blue's skin. Peaceful clamped down. He gritted his teeth and shut his eyes and jerked as hard as he could.

"Neigh!" Ole Blue screamed.

"Did ya get it? Did ya get it, boy?" Dr. Sutherland shouted.

Peaceful felt Ole Blue's foreleg hit him in the shoulder. He fell to the ground from the force of the kick. He could hear Ole Blue rearing and stomping, but he held onto the forceps with both hands.

"Did he kick you, boy, did he kick you?" Dr. Sutherland rushed forward with the candle and lantern.

Peaceful raised his hands holding the forceps. He lay on the ground, looking at the huge long jagged splinter with blood dripping from the sharp end. Peaceful just smiled as he looked at the bloody splinter. "I got it! I got it!" Peaceful rolled and climbed to his knees, studying the bloody splinter.

"Did he kick you, boy, did he kick you?" Dr. Sutherland asked.

Peaceful grinned at Dr. Sutherland, "Yeah, he kicked me, but it didn't hurt; didn't hurt a bit."

"I thought he was gonna stomp you to death."

"Naw, not ole Peaceful. He wasn't stompin'; he was just tellin' me it hurt."

Dr. Sutherland leaned over, studying the bloody

105

splinter. Then he straightened up. "We're gonna have to catch that horse. He's bleedin' like a stuck hog. We'll have to cauterize that wound."

Peaceful climbed to his feet, handed the forceps to Dr. Sutherland, and brushed the dust off his pants. "Naw, I don't think Ole Blue'll take to cauterizing. He don't take very kindly to fire or anything hot."

"We're gonna have to stop that blood." Dr. Sutherland set his black bag on the ground and put the forceps inside. "If he won't let you cauterize it, you'd **better get some black ashes and rub it in. That'll stop the blood.**"

"Thank you, Dr. Sutherland." Peaceful stuck his hand out and shook hands with Dr. Sutherland with both hands. "I'll stop that blood with black ashes. I wanna thank you for saving his life. He's the best friend I got in the whole world."

"Son, I didn't do anything; you did it all." Dr. Sutherland took his black bag in one hand and the candle in the other hand. He left the lantern for Peaceful and walked away muttering, "Damn Mexicans shot all day long fer four days now, and all they could hit was a horse."

"Mr. Mitchell, we thought since your horse has been wounded and all, you wouldn't mind if we shot him and had him for supper tonight." Jerry Day, the Missouri cook scowled at Peaceful and scratched his teeth with a toothpick.

"Eat my horse?" Peaceful grabbed the cook's shirt. "You mean eat Ole Blue?" He shook the cook's shirt.

"Well, he's all shot up." The cook raised his butcher-knife as he looked at Peaceful's grip on his shirt. "He ain't gonna be fit to ride. He's got a lot of torn muscles in that front leg. We don't have any hay to feed him, and it just occurred to me that the best thing we could do would be to shoot him and eat him."

"Eat my horse!" Peaceful grabbed the knife sharpener with one hand and the butcher knife with the other hand and jerked them away from the cook. "They ain't nobody gonna eat Ole Blue."

"Well I just thought the boys would like a little

change of vittles around here, and I thought maybe a little horsemeat..." The cook cut his eyes toward the butcher knife which Peaceful was now holding by the handle not far from his throat. The cook stopped talking and started staring at the butcher-knife near his throat.

"Nobody's gonna ever eat Ole Blue. If he was to die, I still wouldn't let nobody eat him. I would bury him just like a member of the family. He may look like a horse to you, but he ain't just a horse to me. He's like a brother, like a member of the family. We've rode through the rains together; we've swam the rivers together; we've turned our backs to wind storms and jumped at the same bolt of lightening. Whatever I've done, he's done. Wherever I've been, he's been. Why, if I met a pretty girl, I wouldn't marry her 'less'n Ole Blue approved of her." Peaceful looked at Day's butcher-knife and knife-sharpener with disapproval. He handed them back to the cook with one hand. "You take your stinkin' ole butcher-knife back to the cook's shed. You can use it cutting up beeves, but don't you even think about using that knife on no horse. They ain't nobody gonna eat Ole Blue, no matter how bad he's shot up."

The cook went on sharpening the butcher knife on the whetstone. "We ain't got no hay to feed him, and he's all shot up."

Peaceful didn't like the way the cook stopped and examined the sharpness of his butcher-knife. "Say another word and I'll shoot you for even thinkin' on it." Peaceful clicked back the hammer on his rifle.

"Oh no." The cook held up both hands, the whetstone in one hand and the butcher-knife in the other hand. He backed away from Peaceful, still holding his hands up in the air. "I never seen anybody so stuck on a horse," he mumbled to himself as he walked back toward the cook's shack, sharpening his butcher-knife as he walked.

22

"Colonel Crockett!" Johnny Ballentine came racing northward along the east wall. He was running and waving his rifle. "Colonel Crockett, I heard two coyote howls. There's some men out there that wants in." He climbed down the ladder at the northeast corner of the wall around the patio. He ran across the patio.

Peaceful rolled out of his blanket and was sitting on his all fours, reaching in the darkness for his rifle.

Crockett was sitting on the edge of his blankets putting on his boots. He plopped his coonskin cap on his head and rose to his feet. He stretched his arms wearily and yawned. "I heard those two sorry howls. They were so sorry they woke me up. Sounds like John W. Smith's back from his trip to Gonzales." Crockett cradled his rifle in his arm and took off behind Ballentine, who led him to the northeast corner of the walled patio.

They climbed the ladder and crawled onto the top of the wall, keeping low until they stood over the north portal.

"They're right out there, Sir." Private Ballentine pointed his rifle toward a thicket of trees about half a mile northeast of the northeast corner of the patio.

Crockett laid his rifle, Old Betsy, down. He turned his head and cupped his hands over his ears, listening.

Peaceful had climbed the wall behind Crockett and had followed him along the north wall. He held his

108

breath and turned his head and his ears to the north-east, listening.

"They's some men out there alright." Crockett was now on his hands and knees. "I can hear their horses, but I can't tell how many there are. Doesn't sound like a very big relief column."

"Do you think it's Colonel Fannin and his men from Goliad?" Ballentine asked.

Crockett shook his head. "No telling who it is. Or how many there are. It smells to me like there's only about thirty horses out there. I'm gonna give 'em a double coyote howl and tell 'em to come on in." Crockett remained on his knees. He threw back his head and cupped his hands over his mouth. Then he let a coyote howl. "Owoou, owoou."

Peaceful shook his head slowly as he admired the authenticity of Crockett's coyote howl. It sounded like a real coyote howling from the top of the Alamo walls.

Crockett's two coyote howls caused horses to bound out of the trees about a half mile to the northeast of the Alamo.

"Somebody get down there and open that gate. We've got a relief column coming in." Then Crockett waved his hand toward Squire Daymon and the other men sitting around the campfire near the pallisade. "I need about a dozen men up here with long-barrelled Kentucky rifles. We're gonna have to be ready to pick off any Mexicans that try to stop that relief column as they come into this north portal."

"How do we know they're ours instead of Mexicans?" Ballentine asked.

Crockett watched as a dozen men with rifles raced for the ladder at the northeast corner of the patio wall. He looked at Johnny Ballentine. "We don't know," he grinned. "We're gonna have to let 'em in and then find out if they're ours or not."

The rumbling of horse hoofs rolled through the hills.

Crockett held up his hand for attention. "I don't want any shots fired. Let's let 'em get in here without any shots bein' fired if we can, 'cause if we start

109

shootin', they ain't gonna know if we're shootin' at them or at Mexicans. So hold your fire til I shoot."

"Sounds like a lot of horses, don't it?" Peaceful spoke to Johnny Ballentine as he moved his head to better catch the sound of the rumbling horses approaching.

"There! I see 'em!" Little Joe Bayliss lowered his rifle and pointed at a thin dark line of horsemen leaning low over their horses' manes.

The blast of a rifle cut the night air. Then another rifle barked, not from the Alamo, but from the Mexican lines.

Crockett held up his hand. "No shootin'." He rose to his feet on top of the wall, attracting attention to his tall, coonskin-capped figure. "if we shoot, we'll just attract attention to them and maybe scare them into slowing down.

"Colonel, you think they might be Mexicans?" Ballentine asked.

"Naw, I don't think they're Mexicans. I don't think any Mexicans would be foolish enough to try to ride into the Alamo, 'specially along this north wall." He stepped backward and leaned over, looking down into the patio. "Is that door open?" he shouted.

"Yes, Sir, standin' open wide. And here they come!"

Peaceful grinned as he looked into the candle-lit inner patio while the sound of horse hoofs became louder and louder. He frowned as the rifle fire on the outside grew in intensity.

Then John W. Smith came racing through the north portal, waving his rumpled white hat as his horse galloped into the inner patio. He was followed by a dusty stream of sweating horses.

Crockett leaned over, looking into the patio, nodding his head, counting the horses as they galloped into the patio. When the stream of horses stopped, Crockett cradled Old Betsy in his arms and looked at Johnny Bellentine. "I counted thirty-one."

"Never fired a shot." Johnny Hayes cradled his rifle in his arm and looked at the horses milling in the patio.

110

"There ain't enough men there to make any difference." Squire Daymon shook his head.

"I don't believe they're all in. Sounds to me like there's another man out there." Crockett turned and cupped his hand to his ear.

"Huh?" Johnny Ballentine turned and stared off to the northeast.

"Yeah, there's another man out there. I can hear him coming toward the portal." Crockett looked down into the patio. "Get that portal door open. There's another man out there, and he's comin' in."

The rider galloped through the portal through a hail of Mexican bullets. He reined hard and fast and jumped off his horse. He ran back to the portal door, shouting, "Don't shut that door! Don't shut that door! My dog's out there!"

Crockett leaned over, looking at the latest arrival. "Look at that. Just a boy. And he hasn't even got a gun." Crockett shook his head. "And he wants us to leave the door open so his dog can get in." He shook his head again. "Some damn relief column. Just some old men and boys from Gonzales."

"Some of 'em don't even have guns," Squire Daymon volunteered.

Crockett cradled Old Betsy in his arm as he climbed down the ladder at the northeast corner of the wall. "This is the first relief column to reach the Alamo. Now that these old men and these boys have got to San Antonio, maybe the next relief contingent will be big enough to make some difference."

"Look at 'em make their way over to our fire. Looks like they didn't bring any groceries," Squire Daymon observed.

"Maybe there'll be another relief column ridin' in by daylight. Hey, I wonder what time of the day this is, anyway?" Crockett reached inside his jacket and pulled out his watch. He squinted as he looked at the time. "It's 3:00 a.m., March the first. If some more men start arriving, we've got a chance to hold this fort yet."

"If them Mexicans don't kill you, I sure will." Tom

111

Miller glared at young Johnnie Kellog, one of the recent arrivals from Gonzales.

"Yeah, I know." Nineteen-year-old Johnnie Kellog fingered the wooden ramrod fastened under his flintlock rifle.

"What you mad at Kellog about?" Peaceful asked as the three men crouched low behind the ramparts of the south wall. "I don't like to hear one man talkin' about killin' another man. You'd have to have a powerful reason 'fore you could take a fellow soldier's life. Private Conway got hung to that big ole pecan tree the day I arrived here on account of shootin' a fellow soldier. You gotta have an awful good reason or you'll hang."

"Kellog stole my wife." Miller blinked his eyes.

"Didn't either. She didn't say I stole her. She saddled her own horse when we rode away. I didn't steal. I didn't steal Anne. She just wanted Johnnie Kellog more than she did Tom Miller.

"Don't make no nevermind. She was my wife. You stole her. I'm going to kill you, an' I'm goin' to enjoy it, watchin' your blood run outta your guts."

"Tom, you been talkin' that way for two days now. You know what your trouble is? You ain't got the guts."

"I have, too."

"I got your wife, an' I got her good, and all you do is talk. I ain't no more afraid of you than I am them Mexicans waiting outside the Alamo fer a good fight."

"You ain't scared, are you, Johnnie?" Miller asked, licking his lips.

"Nope, I shore ain't, but I can tell you are."

"I don't believe you are scared, Johnnie, else you wouldn't have rode seventy miles from Gonzales to be here, not with me sitting there riding beside you, hating your guts, with a loaded gun in my hand. I should have shot you that first night out."

"You can't shoot; you're a coward. You ain't never caught me with an empty gun. You're a damn coward."

Tim Miller shook his head, but he didn't say a word.

112

23

"Colonel, what're we gonna do about them playin' them bugles and beatin' them drums in the middle of the night like they're fixin' to attack the fort?" Peaceful asked Colonel Crockett.

"Them bugles makin' you a little nervous, Lad?"

Peaceful nodded his head.

"Well maybe we better make a little music and make them nervous." Crockett grinned at the thought. "Where's McGregor and his Scottish bagpipes?"

"Oh, McGregor's over in the artillerymen's quarters." Little Joe Bayliss put down the rifle he was oiling and cleaning. "I heard him play that durn thing down by the river the other day, and he scared ever' bird on the river. Rabbits took off for tall timber and the squirrels tried to cover their ears with their tails, and when that didn't work, they took off for the tallest trees they could find. Them bagpipes sound awful if you ain't never heard 'em before. I believe they'd stop a chargin' herd of Comanche Indians and send 'em home to hide under their squaw's bed."

"We'll what're we waiting for? Let's get ole McGregor out here with them bagpipes and give them Mexicans a taste of their own medicine." Davy Crockett grinned.

The moon was three hands high. Cannon shells were whistling into the Alamo and bouncing around the stone walls. Fifteen-year-old William E. King of Gonzales was running around chasing the cannonballs down and carrying them over his shoulder to Lieutenant Dickerson, who handled the eight-and twelve-pound cannons along the north wall. Billy King carried the cannon shells smiling a toothy grin that crackled his frecked face. His smile said he was glad he was carrying the shells and piling them up by Dickerson's cannons, knowing they'd be fired back at the Mexicans. Every cannon shell caused Billy to straighten up and listen to the whistle, trying to determine where that shell would fall, how far he would have to run to chase it down and carry it to Lieutenant Dickerson. Billy was listening to a cannon shell whistle its way to the Alamo when he heard a shrill, awful racket that ran chills up and down his spine.

"What on earth is that?" Johnny Hays threw back the blanket from around his head.

Peaceful looked down from his guard post on the south wall and spotted McGregor's white beard sparkling in the moonlight. Peaceful thought he could see a smile on the old man's face. McGregor twirled his fingers, getting a shrill and awesome music from his leather bagpipes. The old man sat still in the center of the inner patio. His head moved slightly to the Scottish music.

The fort grew suddenly silent. From his guard post at the top of the wall, Peaceful could hear a babble of Mexican voices jabbering alarm in the cover of willows along the San Antonio River. Peaceful moved in that direction as the Mexican jabber grew louder and louder and the Mexican cannons stopped firing. It was quiet on both sides of the river, except for Crockett's fiddle, Ballantine's guitar, and McGregor's bagpipes! Peaceful could almost see the Mexicans turning their heads, trying to make out the nature of this new shrill, ominous sound coming from within the walls of the Alamo.

From his perch at the southwest corner of the fort, Peaceful nodded his head at the sudden silence. There was no sound in the night air other than McGregor's militant Scottish tune, Ballentine's quiet guitar, and Crockett's out-of-tune fiddle.

114

Peaceful heard voices gathering along the east bank of the chalk river. He could make out the caps of two Mexican officers. He recognized one as being the soldier who had ridden up close to the fort carrying a white flag the day Santa Anna arrived. He was the handsome Colonel Almonte who had ridden with Colonel Bowie. Peaceful saw him pushing willows aside and turning his head, listening to the shrill bagpipe music. Colonel Almonte turned to a heavy-set officer who was sticking his head through the willows beside the colonel. "General Woll, did you ever hear anything like that before?" Colonel Almonte asked.

"Ja," General Woll nodded his head. "I heard this British sound at Waterloo."

"It's frightening, isn't it?" Colonel Almonte stared at the stone walls of the Alamo.

"Ja. I was with General Bleucher at Waterloo. This horrible music frightened us then, even though they were on our side of the line." He turned to Colonel Almonte. "The British and Germans fought together at Waterloo. We managed to whip the French, but we always trembled at the sound of those bagpipes."

"What does the playing of the bagpipes mean?" Almonte asked.

"The British are coming." General Woll shook his head.

Colonel Almonte stared at General Woll. "The British are coming?" he asked.

"Ja! Either the British are coming, or else there's a Scottsman about." General Woll turned in the willows and marched away.

"A Scottsman!" Colonel Almonte gasped. "Maybe the British *are* coming." He shut his eyes and put his hands over his ears as he stalked unhappily back to the Mexican lines.

24

It was daylight. The sun was just coming up over the eastern hills. Peaceful stirred uneasily in his blanket, welcoming the warmth of daylight.

Peaceful jumped up at the sound of a rifle being fired at the wall right above his head. He tossed aside his blanket and grabbed his rifle and quickly clambered to his feet. "What happened? What happened?"

Then Peaceful saw Colonel Crockett standing straight up, not hiding behind the wall, standing stiff and straight, reloading his rifle.

"Did you get one, Colonel?" Peaceful asked.

"Sure did. That makes six I've sent to the cemetery since Santa Anna arrived."

"Colonel, I wanna ask you something." Peaceful walked over close to Colonel Crockett as he spoke. "Why do you stand up straight when you shoot?"

"What'd'ya mean, Peaceful?"

"I don't understand why you stand up after you shoot, making such a target of yourself."

"Aw, I don't know." Crockett rubbed Old Betsy fondly after he had loaded her. "I guess I stand up straight after I shoot to make sure I didn't miss. I know the man I shot at ain't gonna be shootin' back," Crockett grinned.

"You don't mind shootin' at all, do you Colonel?" Peaceful asked.

"Naw, of course not. Do you have trouble shooting?"

116

"I don't know if I have any trouble or not; I ain't shot nobody yet."

"Well, you haven't had a chance; you haven't had the opportunity," Crockett suggested.

"Naw, that ain't right, Colonel. I had a chance; I could've shot a man last night."

"You mean you had a shot and didn't take it?" Crockett asked.

"Yeah, you remember last night when you and McGregor was playin' them bagpipes?"

Crockett nodded.

"Well, I saw a couple of Mexican officers down there in the willows. They was talking about how scarey them bagpipes was. I could hear 'em talkin', and I believe I could've shot 'em."

"You ain't never killed a man, have you, Peaceful?"

Peaceful shook his head.

"The first killin's always the hardest. After that, it gets easier and easier."

"I could've killed last night," Peaceful turned and looked askance at Crockett, "but I didn't."

"Well, they weren't shootin' at you. You wait til a bullet grazes your forehead. You'll find shootin' back comes mighty natural like."

"I don't know about that." Peaceful looked to the west where Mexican soldiers were dragging away the body of the man Crockett had just shot. "I've seen you shoot two men, and I still don't have no stomach for it."

"What's the matter, Peaceful? You tryin' to tell me you can't shoot?"

"All I know is that I ain't shot yet."

"Well, there ain't been nobody shot in here, either." Crockett turned and studied the stone walls of the Alamo. "When the bullets start flyin', you'll find your appetite for shootin'."

"I don't know." Peaceful stared across the river at the dead man's heels bobbing in the grass as he was being drug away.

Johnny Hays came walking down the wall, rubbing his belly, a satisfied grin on his face. "Thanks,

117

Colonel, for spelling me for breakfast." He pointed to the west toward the river. "Hay, did you get one while I was gone?" he asked.

Crockett nodded.

"Well, I'll be dad-burned. I wonder why I didn't see him." Johnny Hayes squinted over the top of the wall.

"It was easy. It was just like picking out which eye of a turkey you wanted to put a bullet through."

"Did you get him between the eyes?" asked Johnny.

Crockett nodded, and Johnny Hayes grinned, but Peaceful didn't. He felt of his forehead and sat down, a little sick at his stomach.

"Don't you wish you could drop 'em like ole Crockett? I understand he's already got six under his belt." Johnny squinted over the top of the wall.

Peaceful felt his head shake. Then Johnny leaned back away from the wall and climbed down beside him.

"Don't you shake your head at Johnny Hays. I know you would like to have six Mexicans under your belt."

Peaceful stared at Johnny, then looked at the four loaded rifles at his station at the wall. Johnny was ready to shoot. Peaceful wondered if he ever would be.

25

"The men from Gonzales brought a letter when they came in. Fact is, they brought several letters." **Johnny Hays ran up to Peaceful. He was far in front of Captain Kimball, who had just arrived with thirty-two men from Gonzales.** "Peaceful, you even got a letter."

"I have a letter!" Peaceful stared at the letter, looking at it, then at Captain Kimball, who was fresh in from Gonzales, and back at the soiled, water-stained, yellowed envelope. "I never got a letter before." He turned his head from side to side as he stared at the envelope being handed him by Captain Kimball, trying to figure out how a letter was opened, what one did to read it.

"Here, don't you want it?" Captain Kimball handed the letter to Peaceful.

Peaceful took the letter in his finger tips and held it out at arm's length, turning it in his fingers. "I got a letter," he spoke quietly to himself.

"Well, ain't you going to open it?" Johnny Hays came up close, leaned over, and sniffed of the envelope. "It smells like leather, like saddle bags. Must be from your girl," Johnny laughed.

Peaceful kept fingering the envelope, feeling of it with his finger tips, turning it over, running his forefinger over the flat side.

"Well, ain't you going to open it?" Johnny looked at the envelope with anxious, envious eyes.

Peaceful shook his head.

"He ain't through feelin' of it!" Squire Daymon folded his arms in the candlelight, "He's feelin' of it like Johnny feels of a woman."

"Yeah, leave him alone." Little Joe Bayliss pushed Johnny Hays back. Let him hug it an' kiss it a couple times. Maybe he-ll read it to us."

"Is it from Tennessee?" Andy Nelson asked.

Peaceful turned his head and looked at Andy.

"Don't you know where it's from?" Little Joe Bayliss' grinning face turned serious.

Squire Daymon reached for the envelope. "You want me to read it to you?" he asked.

Peaceful stopped fingering the envelope, brought it to his ear, listening, then held it at arm's length, studying it silently. He pulled it to his chest protectively for a silent second. He turned slowly to Squire Daymon and nodded his head.

"You want me to read it here, or off to ourselves?"

Peaceful shrugged his shoulders.

"Maybe we better go to the Officers' Quarters and read it by lamplight." Squire Daymon nodded his head toward the privacy of the quiet Officers' Quarters.

"Oh no you don't!" Johnny Hays grabbed at the envelope. "That letter's from Tennessee; we got a right to hear what it says."

Squire Daymon jerked the envelope out of Johnny's grip. "It's Peaceful's letter. I'll read it where he says read it." Squire Daymon turned his back to Johnny Hays and held the letter high in the air.

"Read it." Peaceful nodded to Squire Daymon.

Squire Daymon lowered the letter slowly, ruffling his broad shoulders at Johnny Hays. He moved over toward the candle-lit table by the north wall. Then he picked up the candle and handed it to Peaceful.

"You hold the candle." He pressed the candle into Peaceful's hand. "If you want me to stop reading, just snuff out the candle."

Peaceful nodded and raised the candle over Squire Daymon's shoulder.

"It's addressed to Napoleon Bonaparte Mitchell."

120

Squire Daymon moved his nose close to the envelope. "Care of the Texas Army. It's been to Memphis, Natchez, New Orleans, Galveston, Nacogdoches, and Washington-on-the-Brazos." Squire Daymon moved the envelope closer to his nose. "It's from Martha Moffit." Squire Daymon took his gaze off the letter and tossed a fat-chinned grin at Peaceful. "That your girlfriend?"

Peaceful shook his head. "That's my girlfriend's mama." Peaceful spoke seriously. Johnny Hays laughed.

"He's got a letter from his sweetheart's mama!" Hays turned his mischievous eyes at Peaceful. "Man, he's in trouble, in big trouble."

"You want me to read it?" Squire Daymon moved his fingers to tear open the envelope.

Peaceful nodded.

Squire Daymon tore open the envelope. "It's just a newspaper clipping." He unfolded the tiny bit of newspaper. It's about a girl's funeral in Belvedere, Tennessee."

Peaceful steeled his jaws.

"You want me to read it to you?"

Peaceful nodded.

"The heading of the article reads, Molly Moffit buried on Shaw Mountain'." Squire Daymon stopped reading. He held the paper at arm's length, staring at it for a minute. Then he raised his gaze and looked over the newspaper clipping at Peaceful Mitchell. His lips moved before words came. "Isn't that..." Squire Daymon shook the paper. "Ain't that your girlfriend?"

Peaceful stiffened. He held out his hand. "Give me the paper."

Squire Daymon handed Peaceful the folded yellow newspaper clipping.

"My Molly's dead." Peaceful took the newspaper clipping and put it inside his jacket pocket next to his heart. He walked away slowly, then turned to Squire Daymon.

"I think my Ma killed my Molly, poisoned her, she

died so quick like, poisoned her to punish Abner Moffit for killing my Pa." Peaceful blinked at squire Daymon. He sniffed sadly, "But look who she punished."

"It hurts, I know it hurts." Squire comforted Peaceful.

Peaceful Mitchell's face wrinkled around the eyes and nose. His body trembled. He reached out one trembly hand, like one feeling for help, a hand raised into the air, toward the sky, like one feeling for the sky, to see if it was going to rain. Peaceful pulled in a low mournful sigh. "I just want to die. I don't want to live. I've travelled like a turtle looking for quicksand."

Squire Daymon placed his big heavy hand on Peaceful's shoulder. "Ah reckon a lot of men come here to the Alamo to die." He motioned toward Crockett at the Pallisade wall. "Crockett just lost an unfair election. He got defeated for Congress fer takin' a right stand. His former friend, President Andy Jackson saw to Crockett's defeat, and Jackson did it 'cause Crockett was allus holding up fer thu Indians, being against takin' thu Indians land an' movin' them west."

Peaceful stared open-mouthed at Squire Daymon. The amazement in his eyes told Squire Daymon to go on, to continue.

"Look at our Commanding Officer, he and his wife got a divorce just this past January, 23rd. He thought his wife had been unfaithful. He's thu one that got thu divorce. He never even asked for his daughter, his youngest child. His wife's one woman what's burned, what's fair scalded that Travis. He shies away from women like a blinded bird that can't see , that's afraid to land, especially not next to no woman."

Peaceful took Squire Daymon's hand and led him over to the burro cart next to the horse stockade and sat on the cart, motioning for Squire Daymon to sit next to him. And kept talking.

"Tell me more." Peaceful asked of the older man.

"Well everybody knows that James Bowie ain't the

122

same man since his wife and two kids died of the cholera. Their sudden death struck Bowie harder'n any bullet what's ever been shot. Bowie's been drinking ever since they died in '32, mighty nigh four years ago. He's beein drinkin' like thu well done run dry. He fights an' drinks like he's tryin' tu kill himself. I 'spect he is."

Peaceful nodded and leaned back on the squeaky burro cart. "Yeah, I reckon I ain't the only one what's lost a loved one."

Squire Daymon spread his hands, waving them to the Alamo patio, waving them as if to point from wall to wall. "The Alamo's full of sad-eyed men, wantin' to die."

26

"I got a girl, and she's red-headed and freckled-faced and as pretty as a white crow." Johnny Ballentine sat with his rifle cradled across his lap, with his black hat pushed back against the south wall. He and Daniel Cloud were sitting on top of the white cottonwood logs that covered the shed room on the south side of the Alamo patio.

"I never seen a white crow." Cloud leaned forward, staring at Johnny Ballentine. He studied Ballentine's eyes for a moment, then winked as a smile grew on Ballentine's face. He followed Johnny's stare down into the patio and saw that Johnny was looking at Susannah Dickerson, who raised up in the firelight from her task of stirring the boiling beef in a huge cast-iron cooking pot near the west wall.

"You're looking at Susannah Dickerson, Lieutenant Dickerson's wife."

Johnny nodded his head and pulled in a deep sigh. "Ain't she the p'rttiest gal you ever saw?"

"Yeah, but she's married. That's Lieutennant Dickerson's wife," Cloud exclaimed as he held out his hands.

"Look, Cloudy Boy, falling in love is like fallin' off a bluff. You don't do it on purpose; you do it accidental. And when you fall, it's done 'fore you know it. They's some men that can pick out who they're gonna fall in love with, an' they's some that can't. I knew she was married, but I couldn't help it. She smiled at me real pr'tty-like one evenin' when she was puttin' hoe cake and boiled beef in my tin plate. I just stood there and looked at her till my food got cold. Johnny Hays had to come over there and lead me a-way and set me down next to the wall. She touched my hand when she handed me that hot plate, and all of a sudden I wasn't hungry." Ballentine had the long, sad face of a cast-out hungry dog.

"You mean you've done gone and fell in love with that..." Cloud pointed at the slender figure of Susannah Dickerson in her blue and white polka-dot dress with a white collar and a blue belt tied in a big bow on the side. Cloud pushed the brim of his hat up for a better look. "She is kinda pr'tty, ain't she?" He pulled the brim of his hat down over his eyes. "But she's a lieutenant's wife, and she's a good woman."

"Yep, she shore is."

"But she's a lieutenant's wife. What'd you fall in love with her for?"

"Sometimes Cupid's arrow falls where it shouldn't."

"How long's this been goin' on?" Cloud asked.

"About a week."

"Have you said anything to her?"

"Nope."

"Does she know?"

"Yep."

"How does she know?"

"Well, she's seen me spill my food, and stumble and trip walkin' on perfectly flat ground, and she's caught me lookin' at her."

"You mean you've fallen in love with a girl and that you've never done nothin' about but just look at her?"

"Yep."

"What'cha gonna do about it?"

"Nothin'."

"You mean you're in love with a lieutenant's wife and you ain't gonna do nothin' about it?"

"That's right, Cloudy Boy. There's somethin' power-fully unselfish about bein' in love with somebody. When you're in love, you want them to love you; you want them to want you. And when you really love somebody, you want them to have what they want,

125

even if it's somebody else."

"Man, you are mixed up."

"Naw, I ain't mixed up. Man, I tell you, she touched me this mornin', and I been feelin' no pain all day. I keep rememberin' how it felt, just to be touched. It was a good feelin'. It was such a good feelin'."

"What you gonna do about Lieutenant Dickerson?"

"Nothin'."

"Nothin'?" Cloud moved his head back and forth with a hesitant, almost disbelieving shake of his head.

"Aw, even if Susannah was single, she might not want me."

"She's got a fifteen-month old baby."

"Yeah, ain't that little Elizabeth pr'tty? She's got her mama's red hair and that light sun-freckled skin."

"You think she's pr'tty?" Cloud asked.

"She ain't just pretty. She's beautiful; she's plum beautiful."

Cloud turned his head and stared down into the patio, surveying the slender red-headed woman in the blue polka dot dress stirring the contents of a stew pot with a long wooden stick, stirring with both hands. She was looking up into the night sky like a woman who was happy, like she was satisfied with what she was doing.

Cloud pulled his hat brim back down over his eyes. "You southern Alabamans are proof that beauty is in the eyes of the beholder."

Later that night, when the patio was still and quiet, and the white walls were lit by soft candlelight, Johnny Ballentine sat in the soft shadow of the south wall, plucking the battered banjo he had brought all the way from Alabama. He sang low and quiet:

"Oh Susannah, don't you cry for me,

I've come from Alabama with my banjo on my knee;

I have come to Texas,

My true love for to see."

Johnny Ballentine sang his song low and mournfully, so quiet that no one heard it but him, and the moon, and the stars.

In the dark shadow of the south wall, no one could see the tears in Johnny Ballentine's eyes, not even the stars, not even the moon.

"Wonder why the Lord left a beautiful woman like Susannah Dickerson locked up here in the Alamo with a hundred and eighty-three lonely, lusty men." Squire Daymon picked his teeth with the long thin blade of a hunting knife.

"The Lord didn't put her in here," Johnny Hays grinned. "General Santa Anna sent her in here to make us want to go where we could be with our wives and sweethearts."

"Aw, Santa Anna had nothin' to do with the Lieutenant's wife," Ballentine spoke sharply. "She moved in here to stay with her husband before Santa Anna ever came on the scene. And besides, nobody but her husband, Lieutenant Almeron Dickerson, can tell her what to do or influence her in any way." Johnny Ballentine had those slow-moving, wistful eyes of a heart-struck man. "She's as pure and faithful as unfailing spring water."

"Listen to the Alabama boy," Johnny Hays scoffed. "He's been bitten by the cupid bug. Don't you know there ain't no such a thing as a faithful woman?"

Johnny Ballentine shook his head slowly, firmly. "Susannah Dickerson wouldn't ever . . . she wouldn't ever . . . she just wouldn't ever do nothin' wrong." Johnny Ballentine sighed, and his eyes continued in that soft, dreamy, far-away silent admiration.

"Susannah Dickerson got locked up with a hundred an' eighty-three men that ain't her husband. She's cookin' for us, she's washin' dishes for us, and she's washin' clothes for us. There's times she almost has to bathe us." Johnny Hays laughed as he thought of the way some of the men washed themselves in the soapy dishwater. "If she could find the privacy, she'd be a wife to ever' one of us. She's a woman. She runs her fingers over her hips and lower belly when nobody's lookin', and there's a gentleness and delicate-

127

ness in the way she does it that makes me think she wishes somebody else was doin' the feelin'."

"Not Susannah." Johnny Ballentine rose to his feet and climbed over Squire Daymon. He kicked Johnny Hays on the foot.

Johnny Hays just lay on his back with his hands folded under his head and grinned. "You don't know women, Ballentine. That woman's been in here nearly two weeks cookin' food and servin' it to a hundred and eighty-three men. You can't tell me she wouldn't like to lay down with somebody besides her husband."

"No!" Johnny Ballentine kicked Hays again. "She wouldn't even think of such a thing."

"Aw, no? Notice how she's always touchin' up her red hair?" Johnny Hays brought his fingers up and touched them delicately around his shoulders, imitating a woman admiring her hair with her fingertips. "And then when she walks, she prisses her hips." Johnny Hays moved his head from side to side, like a woman who knows what she's got and ain't ashamed of it.

"You say one more word about Susannah Dickerson, and you'll have this Alabama boy to answer to."

"Aw, I wouldn't duel you, Johnny." Johnny Hays waved away the idea with a broad sweep of his hand. "You act like you're in love with the woman."

Johnny Ballentine nodded his head slowly as he stared at the ground. "I am."

27

At dusk on the fifth of March, after a big hole had
been breeched in the south wall, the cannonading
from the Mexicans in San Antonio stopped. An
ominous silence rose in the fort. Sergeant Ward was
suddenly sober. He rose from his gun mounts on the
eighteen-pounder at the southwest corner of the
Alamo. He raised his powder-blackened head high in
the air and cupped his powder-blackened hand over
his good ear. "What's that I hear?"

Cherokee Campbell from Tennessee put on his Indian grin. "That's silence you hear."

"You sure that's silence?" Sergeant Ward asked,
raising his head higher in the air and turning his ear.
"Sounds awful, don't it?"

Cherokee Campbell didn't say anything. He just
smiled at the godly, peaceful silence, enjoying it for
the first time in eleven days.

"I thought I had lost my hearing; I thought I was
stone deaf." Sergeant Ward rubbed his ears and
listened again. "I never thought silence could sound
like that." He shook his head. "And be so scarey."

Cherokee Campbell stared at the blackened wiping
cloth. "Even wild animals tremble with fear in
silence. I've seen deer tremble and shake just before I
shot 'em."

"Maybe we're deer just fixing to get shot." Sergeant
Ward leaned on his ramrod.

Peaceful lowered the butt of his rifle to the ground

and stared over the west wall toward San Antionio. He could hear a rooster crowing in a chicken coop across the San Antonio River. "Did you hear that rooster crow?" Peaceful asked Sergeant Ward.

Sergeant Ward nodded.

"That proves you ain't deaf." Peaceful grinned.

Sergeant Ward nodded again.

"Don't that sound odd after all the cannoneering and rifle shots and bugle calls in the middle of the night? Imagine a rooster after all that racket."

"Maybe they're fixing to leave; maybe they're fixing to move out," Sergeant Ward smiled.

"They won't leave now. They've busted a hole in the south wall." Cherokee Campbell squinted in the darkening twilight, trying to make out the hole blasted in the south wall near the artillarymen's quarters. "They might have left if we had got reinforcements from Goliad. But they know what we know. Jim Bonham came in from Goliad. Fannin ain't coming."

The silence was broken by a strong voice coming from the inner patio. "This is Colonel Travis. I want all ablebodied men not needed for guard duty to assemble in the patio."

Peaceful stared at Sergeant Ward, and then at Cherokee Campbell. "I'm a guard." Peaceful bit his lips. "I'll have to stay on guard duty."

"I imagine we're going to prayer meeting," Sergeant Ward growled and wiped his hands on the wiping cloth. He started down the gun parapet toward the inner patio.

Cherokee Campbell started to lay his rifle down against the wall, but he thought better of it and put it over his shoulder. He followed Sergeant Ward down the parapet.

Peaceful shouldered his rifle and started walking down the wall, making his weary march, sniffing the pure air, suddenly cleansed of the sulphur smoke of gunpowder. Peaceful stopped his marching and sat down and leaned back against the wall when he saw Colonel Travis mount a barrel. A candle lit the patio.

"I have a few words, Gentlemen," Colonel Travis began with his arms outstretched, like a preacher pleading at the end of his sermon. "I know this is March and you have not been paid since last October. I am fortunate to have even one man. I have deceived you." Travis had his head raised high in the air, and it looked like his eyes were closed. "I have kept your spirits high with the hope that we would be relieved by Fannin's garrison at Goliad. I deceived not only you, but myself, too, for I believed Fannin would come. Jim Bonham has returned from Goliad with word that Fannin is not coming to the relief of the Alamo. Now I know the truth, and the truth is that he is not coming. We stand alone, and we will not be relieved. We are now faced with a decision." Travis lowered his arms. His sign of pain could be heard throughout the Alamo. "Only two choices face us. We can stand and fight, or we can run. I'm going to ask you to vote on which action we are to take. Before you vote, I must tell you this. I was sent here by Governor Smith with specific instructions to destroy the Alamo. I must also tell you that Colonel Bowie was sent here by General Houston with instructions to destroy the Alamo. We did not carry out our instructions. We walked around these walls. We elected to stay and fight. We ask no man to stay with us whose heart tells him to do otherwise." Travis drew his sword and held it high in the night air. "I shall draw a line in the sand of this holy patio, and I shall step across that line. I ask that those who wish to stand and fight with me step across that line with me and all those who do not step across will be free to leave. I pray that God will guide you in your decision." Travis stepped down from the barrel and walked sharply to the west. He stuck his sword in the ground and walked eastward, scratching a line in the sand with his sword as he marched. He stopped and placed his sword back in his scabbard and stepped across the line to the north, leaving all of his men on the south side of the line. Travis stood stiffly, eyeing his men. "Those who wish to stand and fight may join me by stepping across this line." He pulled his sword out and pointed at the line.

"There's 4,000 Mexican troops out there and there's only 183 of us Texans. When they attack in force, we know what is going to happen. We will lose. We will all die. But it is possible to win even in losing. If we fight like Tennesseans and Alabamans and Scotchmen and Texans always fight, and fight long enough and hard enough, we can make this such an expensive victory that Santa Anna's army may win here, but be unable to win another battle in Texas. This is what I ask you to fight for. I ask you to stand with me and die in such a way that we win victory in death."

Peaceful saw a stirring in the lines of men as they looked about for guidance. Then Davy Crockett shouldered his rifle and stepped across the line, followed by his Tennessee Mounted Volunteers. Suddenly, the whole line moved, until only two figures remained on the south side. Peaceful saw James Bowie lying on his cot on the south side of the line. Bowie raised up on one elbow. "Colonel, I can't walk across that line. I'd be much obliged if you'd have some boys move me across." Peaceful watched four men step back across the line and lift Bowie's cot. Little Joe Bayliss, Robert Campbell, another Tennessean, Squire Daymon, and the old chicken man, Johnny Hays, each had a corner of Bowie's cot. They carried him across the line and set him down gently and stepped away.

Bowie raised on his cot and looked back across the line at the only figure that still stood immobile on the south side of the line. Everybody stared at Luis Moses Rose.

"You seem not ready to die with us, Rosie boy." Bowie's voice was strong and clear, not accusative.

"No, I am not ready to die." Rose leaned on his rifle. "Moses Rose has already died once. I died in the retreat of Napoleon's Army from Moscow. God let me live through that. I lived by retreat. I didn't come to Texas to die; I came to Texas to live."

"Even if you escape, Rosie boy, even if you get over

the wall, you'll be caught," Bowie argued.

"Not me," Rose felt of his dark hair. "I speak Spanish and I have dark hair and dark skin. Moses Rose could pass as a Mexican even before Santa Anna himself." Rose stood beside his rifle, remaining on the south side of the line.

"I don't know whether I wish you luck or not." Bowie turned his back to Moses Rose.

Rose laid down his rifle and stared at it for a second. He straightened up and wiped the sand off his hands, then walked around the line. He went into the artillarymen's quarters. He came out with a packet of clothes. He climbed the escarpment to the wall and dropped his packet of clothes on the other side. Rose climbed over the wall and disappeared into the night.

The assembly in the patio remained still and motionless, watching Rose climb over the wall and disappear into the night. Until he dropped his clothes over the wall, Peaceful didn't think he would really leave. As Luis Moses Rose disappeared over the side of the wall, Peaceful felt an urge to raise his rifle and shoot. He wondered what emotion made him want to shoot. Was it cowardice or was is courage? Peaceful wondered.

28

In the silence of the night of the 5th of March, Peaceful felt a strange attraction draw him toward the saintly white stone walls of the Alamo Chapel. The old stones drew him like a shepherd's bell calling and calming a herd of sheep. They tolled not only Peaceful, but many others, toward the candlelight's soft glow. Inside the chapel, Peaceful saw sixteen-year-old Galba Fuqua kneeling before the cross on his knees, the bottoms of his bare feet shaking against the stone floor, his head bowed and nodding in silent prayer, tears streaming down his young cheeks. Peaceful patted him gently on the shoulders, then stared at the candle-lit white cross on the north wall. It had been worn and battered by time. There was a comforting holiness about the splintered cross. It was lit by a strange light. The candles in the roofless church cast a saintly light. Stars shone down through the roofless chapel, giving it second illumination, a godly light that was holy and pure, a pleasant light that lent saintly shadows to the humble men bowed in prayer below the cross.

Peaceful slipped to his knees slowly, staring at the battered old cross gently lit by some light from above. He closed his eyes and put his hands together under his chin. Peaceful tried to pray, but words didn't come. A gentleness settled over his shoulders, a warm comfortable feeling as if a hand from above had patted him on the shoulder, much like when he patted tearful Galba Fuqua on the shoulder and Galba comforted his hand when Galba sniffed and bravely blinked back tears in his young prayer on the cold stone floor.

Peaceful felt better as he patted young Galba on the shoulders again as he rose to leave. He walked across the quiet, candle-lit room and stood silently staring through the broken rafters, looking at the bright stars above. He wondered if there was anyone up there watching. A star seemed to twinkle. Peaceful sighed and left the chapel.

Peaceful walked to the east, toward the pallisade, through the gate, and into the inner patio. He was still looking at the stars when he saw a lantern on a table beside a cot outside Jim Bowie's room along the south wall. He took his eyes off the stars and started walking toward the lantern-lit cot. Peaceful stopped, and he could hear Jim Bowie's voice loud and clear.

"This is my last will and testament."

Peaceful saw Green B. Jameson writing down Bowie's last will.

"I lost my wife, my Beloved Ursula, and my smiling dark-haired son, James, and my pretty blue-eyed daughter, Maria, to the cholera in Montclava, Mexico in 1832. They are buried at the Viramindi Ranch in Montclava, Mexico. The only family I have left is my mother and my three brothers. I appoint my brother, Rezin Bowie, to divide my property equally between my brothers, share and share alike. When the Lord has already taken your wife and your two children, then dying seems like a natural and ordinary thing to do. I have nothing else to say."

Peaceful walked quietly around the lantern-lit cot. He walked past the south portal to the guardhouse on the east side of the south portal. He sat down and leaned his back against the guardhouse door, listening to Jim Bowie dictate his last will. It was witnessed by Green B. Jameson and Thomas Miller. Peaceful was still watching when Thomas Miller, the richest man in Gonzales, began dictating his will. Peaceful wondered if he should make his will. He looked up at

135

the stars thoughtfully. He shrugged his shoulders, then spoke to the stars quietly.

"That's why I'm here; I don't have anything to leave in a will."

A star twinkled. Its twinkle reminded him: "If you die in the Texas Army, you will be entitled to a whole section of land."

Peaceful stared across the patio. He wondered if Green Jameson would let him dictate his will. He walked toward Green B. Jameson at his candle-lit table beside Bowie's cot. Thomas Miller had finished his will and it was being signed and witnessed. Peaceful touched the long lean lawyer on the shoulder. "Mr. Jameson, can I dictate my will?"

"Why yes, son. If the paper holds out, I'll write wills all night."

Jim Bowie patted an empty spot on the edge of his cot. "Sit down, Peaceful. Sit down and tell the Lord and ole Jameson what you want in your will." Bowie reached over and placed Peaceful's hand in his and squeezed it tight. "Will-making time is when all men are the same age."

Green Jameson turned to Peaceful. "Well, I've got written down, 'Know All Men By These Presents.' Now you tell me what you want in your will."

Peaceful looked up at the stars, then looked at long slender Green Jameson, then at Jim Bowie. He gulped. "I ain't never made a will before, and I ain't got nothin' to will."

Jim Bowie laughed.

Green Jameson raised his quill and dipped it in the ink pot and raised it up high. "If we win this here war, you'll be awarded a section of land. That's six hundred forty acres. You might be richer than you think."

"If I die and am entitled to any money or am awarded any land, I want it to be turned into money. I want the money to be used to move me to my girl in Tennessee, or to move my girl's body from Tennessee to me. And if there's any money left, I want a stone memorial set over our graves. I wanna ask the Lord to see that we're together in death as we were in life—that's all I gotta say." Peaceful turned and looked at Green Jameson, who was still writing. Then he looked at Jim Bowie. Bowie was nodding his head. "Is that a will?" Peaceful asked.

Bowie nodded his head again. "Sweetest will I ever heard."

"Never drew a better one." Green Jameson laid the paper on the table near the lantern. "Sign your name right under that last line."

Peaceful took the quill and dipped it in the ink pot. He signed his name, "Napoleon Bonaparte (Peaceful) Mitchell."

Green Jameson and James Bowie witnessed Peaceful's will.

Peaceful Mitchell smiled at the stars as he returned to his post along the pallisade at the south wall of the Alamo. He winked at a blinking star and nodded acceptance as he thought of what tomorrow might bring.

Peaceful wondered if there'd ever be a memorial for the men in the Alamo. He thought that now that he had made his will maybe there would.

29

"I think it's time some young men carried messages from the Alamo." Travis spoke to the six youngsters assembled before his desk in the stone walled Officers' Quarters. Travis leaned over his desk, staring at Billy King. "Billy, do you want to carry a message to Gonzales?"

Billy shook his head. "I came here to fight, not to...not to leave when the going gets rough."

"Do you think a fifteen-year-old boy should stay in the Alamo? Don't you think he should be allowed to ride for home when he's surrounded by four thousand Mexican soldiers?"

"Nope, I think when he's outnumbered, he ought to stay. To stand an' fight."

"You wouldn't go home if I ordered you to?"

"If you ordered."

"How about you, Galba? You're only sixteen; don't you think you should go home?"

"My home was in Gonzales, but now it is here-here in the Alamo. I live wherever I am. I guess I live in San Antonio."

"Why did you step across the line? Why didn't you climb the wall and go home like Moses Rose?"

Galba Fuqua shook his head. "I don't know." He shrugged his thin shoulders. "When Colonel Crockett stepped across the line, he showed he was a man. I had to prove I was a man, too. I had to cross when Colonel Crockett did."

"But I'm giving you a chance to go. To go home. To go as a messenger." Colonel Travis slapped the top of his desk for emphasis.

"Thank you." Galba nodded his head. "Thank you, Sir, but I have no message to carry to San Antonio, an' I can't return to Gonzales and leave my friends here."

"Well, how about you, Johnny Gaston? You're sixteen and from Gonzales, too. Wouldn't you like to carry a message home to Gonzales?"

"Not if I go by myself. Not unless every'body from Gonzales was travelling home, too."

Colonel Travis shook his head. "Isn't there any of you young men who..." Travis stared into young faces, but he saw he was looking into proud manly eyes. "How about you, Peaceful? Aren't you 17, maybe you'll like...? Wouldn't you like to...?"

Peaceful shook his head. "I couldn't carry a message to Belvidere, Tenneesee," Peaceful grinned, "an' I'd be ashamed to hold my head up if I did. I came to Texas to join the army." Peaceful looked down at his feet, avoiding Travis' eyes." I guess I came here to die. I didn't come all the way to Texas to run. I came to join up and serve my time and accept whatever the Lord laid on my plate, an' I'm here an' they're out there." Peaceful jerked his hand toward the Mexican soldiers on the other side of the river. "I plan to stay here till they ain't no Mexican soldiers. So if you're lookin' for a man that wants to go home 'cause of his age, well, I ain't the man. Besides, I'm from Tennessee. We don't never run."

"But I understood you're..." Travis licked his lips, "that you're peaceful, that you don't believe in violence or fighting."

"I seen my pa killed, shot through the head over a tiny strip of land, in an argument with a neighbor over which oak tree was the 'boundry' oak." Peaceful sighed. "I don't believe in takin' somebody's property by force or by fighting. That I don't believe in. At least, I didn't believe in it when I crossed the Sabine River. But you know, Colonel, there's something

139

about this Texas land. I don't know whether it's the sand or these old stones in these walls or whether it's the chalky water we drink." Peaceful smiled and licked his lips. "If you ever drink this Texas water an' it gets in your blood, you become a Texan, or at least proud you're from Tennessee, the Volunteer State, an' that means you never run from a fight. Besides, I'm kinda sad-faced like Jim Bowie. I got just as many reasons to die as I have to live. I'm ready to die."

Dolphin Floyd shook his head when Travis looked at him. "Besides, Colonel, I was twenty-one today. This is my birthday. A man don't want to ride a horse on his birthday. Might fall off an' break a leg or get hurt somethin' awful. I'd rather stay here."

Johnnie Kellog shook his head. "I'm nineeen and another Gonzales man. I ain't leavin'."

Sixteen-year-old Jim Allen saluted Colonel Travis. "Colonel, I'm sixteen. My brother, Poe Allen, he's stayin'. He asked me to go home and tell Mama that Poe's alright, that he did the right thing."

"That sounds like a good message. You carry that message to your mother. You saddle up and get outa here quick like." Travis paused and thought on his words. "Tell your Ma and Pa that Poe Allen did the right thing and that you did too in going home to tell them of your brave brother. You better go tonight while you can."

"Yes, Sir." Jim Allen saluted Travis. "But I ain't got no saddle. I rode in here bare-back. I guess I'll have to ride out that way."

"Wish you luck, Jim." Travis waved as Jim Allen left the room to go home.

Travis dismissed the young men, and Peaceful walked out into the Alamo plaza. He spied gray-headed Robert McGregor. "You're the bagpipe player." He stopped and stood over the white-haired man. "Colonel Travis was just wantin' to know how old ever'body is all of a sudden like. How old are you?"

"I'm Robert McGregor, a fifty-one-year-old Scotchman, recently from Virginia, the oldest private in the New Orleans Grays." McGregor sat on the ground beside Peaceful next to the fire. "I contend I'm the oldest man in the Alamo. Colonel Travis is twenty-six, and Bowie and Crockett are fifty, but there's nobody else in this garrison who can say he's fifty-one."

"You proud you're the oldest man here?" Peaceful asked.

"Well, I don't know about bein' proud. I just know it's a lot easier to die when you're fifty-one than when you're fifteen, like William King."

"Is Billy King just fifteen?" Peaceful asked.

"Yep, he's the youngest an' I'm the oldest." Robert McGregor held out his arms and warmed his hands at the fire.

"Is it easier to die when you're fifty-one than when you're seventeen?" Peaceful turned and looked at the gray-headed man beside him.

"The Lord takes you at all ages, Son. It ain't ever easy to go. It ain't ever easy. But when you've got a half a century under your belt, and you can see the Lord beckoning his finger, I think it's a little easier to follow Him into the other world."

30

"Colonel Crockett, if you will indicate where you and your volunteers wish to make your stand, I will honor your wishes." Colonel Travis stood in the center of the inner patio, his legs set wide apart, his hands folded behind his back, one hand clinging to a sheaf of papers showing the assignment of troups for the final defense of the Alamo.

Crockett had one arm crossed over the top of the barrel of his rifle and the other arm steadying the rifle against his body about belt high. He stood as if his rifle, Old Betsy, was part of his body, a part that could be leaned on, depended on.

"Wal, Colonel, you know we're from Tennessee. We'd be insulted if we were assigned any easy wall to defend. All I ask is that you pick the hardest spot, the toughest wall to defend. Tell me where you think your weakest wall is located. You turn that weak spot over to Davy Crockett and his Tennessee Volunteers and I promise you one thing-nobody'll climb that wall without a hole in his head." Crockett held up one finger and pointed at the center of his forehead. "Right between the eyes."

"Well now," Travis rubbed his chin, "being from Tennessee, you want the toughest spot?" Travis asked.

Crockett nodded his head.

"Well, the weakest spot in our defense will be trying to defend that wooden pallisade. I'd hate to assign anybody to defend a flimsy wood wall of poles and cow skins."

"We will take the pallisade. We'd be offended if we got any other assignment. We'll take the pallisade and I promise you this-no Mexican will ever take it. If Santa Anna ever gets into the Alamo, it won't be by storming Davy Crockett's pallisade between the chapel and the south wall. If he gets in here, it will be at our backs, not from the direction our rifles are pointing."

Travis smiling proudly walked eastward across the patio. "Me and my men will defend the north wall, the wall with the hole in it."

Colonel Travis walked into the quiet chapel, bowing and nodding to the women huddled together, clinging to the east wall.

"How are you this evening, Mrs. Dickerson?" He nodded to Susannah Dickerson, wife of Lieutenant Almeron Dickerson.

Susannah Dickerson nodded and bowed her head, but kept her hands together, staring at the weathered old cross on the wall.

Colonel Travis felt of the gold ring on his finger. He spoke to Mrs. Dickerson. "I have made my will, Mrs. Dickerson, but I find I have one treasured possession I forgot to..." he attempted a smile. "I have this gold ring, given to me by my mother on my wedding day." He took the ring off his finger and studied it for an instant. He pulled a big lungfull of air into his chest. "I was wondering if you'd mind if I gave it to little Elizabeth." Travis stepped forward to hand the ring to the little daughter of Almeron and Susannah Dickerson. Elizabeth stepped backward, hiding her body behind her mother, but peeking around her mother's hip at Colonel Travis.

"Here, let me put it on a string so you can wear it around your neck." Travis cut a rawhide thong from a box on the floor of the chapel. He tied the thong into a loop after running it through the ring. He reached his hand out to little Elizabeth and placed the string around her neck. He watched as she reached up and touched the gold ring.

143

"Wear that ring at your wedding, Elizabeth, or give it to your husband. You'll have more need of it than I will." Travis rose from his knees and strode out of the Alamo Chapel, toward the inner patio.

31

Peaceful returned to his Guard Duty, but Major Baugh, the Officer of the Guard, shook his head. "We'll only need four men on Guard Duty tonight, one on each wall. They're sleepin', gettin' ready for the assault." He nodded his head toward the Mexican lines. "It'll come with the first grey streaks of daylight. No need in you standin' 'round watchin' an' waitin'. You're one of Crockett's men, ain't you?"

Peaceful nodded.

"Well, he's been assigned the wooden pallisade. He demanded the toughest place to defend. That sounds like a Congressman from Tennessee, doesn't it?"

Peaceful nodded.

"Well, you better trot over there and see if you can round up three or four rifles. You'll need all you can get. We're gonna see what hell's like once it gets daylight." He patted Peaceful on the shoulder as Peaceful took off in a slow walk toward the wood pole and cowhide pallisade wall between the chapel and the south wall of the patio.

Peaceful studied his rifle as he walked. He hoped there weren't any more rifles. What he wanted was not another rifle. He stared up at the stars. What he wanted in his hands was not a rifle. He wanted a Bible. He wondered what would happen if he walked out the south portal with a Bible held high in his hands. Was it too late to stop the killing?

Then he saw Crockett standing near the west end of the pallisade, leaning against the southeast corner of

145

the stone chapel. His legs were set apart, leaning a-
gainst the wall. He was clinging to his rifle, Old
Betsy, the back of his coonskin cap barely touching
the wall.

One look at Crockett told Peaceful it was too late for
any Bible. There were three other long-barrelled rifles
leaning against the pallisade, their butts on the
ground, neatly stacked at his feet. There was a silent
grin on his face as he waited for daylight. He was
looking forward to the struggle, the fight, the blood-
shed, grinning as he contemplated how many Mexicans he would kill before he was bayonetted to death.

Peaceful saluted a gentle nod at Crockett. "Colonel
Crockett, I was taken off Guard Duty by Major
Baugh. He told me I should stand with you and the
Tennessee boys here at the Pallisade."

"You mighty right you stand with Crockett's boys.
They ain't no Mexicans gonna climb over our pallisade, are they Mr. Napoleon Bonaparte Mitchell?" He
stepped away from the wall and pounded Peaceful
on the shoulder. "We're gonna stand 'em off, ain't we,
Tennesee boy?"

"I hope so." Peaceful glanced around, studying the
rifles leaning against the wood and cowhide wall. "Is
it alright if I just use my own rifle?"

"I reckon so." Crockett eyed Peaceful and his one
rifle. "If that's what you shoot best with, then that's
what you oughta use."

"Thank you, Sir." Peaceful carried his rifle in one
hand and started to sit down and lean his back a-
gainst the pallisade. Then he noticed his clear spot
was between Hays and Little Joe Bayliss.

They were asleep, with their backs leaning against
the wall and their hands drooped to the sleepy side of
their shoulders.

Peaceful got up slowly, careful not to wake them. He
didn't want to fight next to Johnny Hays. He moved
on down the line and leaned back against the wall between Cherokee Campbell and Squire Daymon.

Squire wasn't asleep. He patted Peaceful on the
knee as Peaceful sat down.

146

"Had any sleep tonight, Peaceful?" he whispered quietly.

"Yeah, I slept a little bit."

"On Guard Duty?"

"No." Peaceful slapped Squire on the shoulder. "Had a couple of hours before I reported, and Major Baugh said we didn't need but four men, one on each wall, and he sent me over here so I could...so I could be with the Tennesee boys."

"So you could die with the Tennessee Volunteers." Squire studied Peaceful's face in the night light. "Isn't that what you started to say?"

Peaceful nodded. Then he spoke. "I hope I don't embarrass nobody." He glanced up and down the pallisade wall.

"From what I heard about your shootin' a whiskey cork out of the air at Washington-on-the-Brazos, you're the best shot here, 'cepting for Colonel Crockett."

"Being a good shot don't make you a good fighter."

"No," Squire Daymon shifted his legs, putting one over the other, "but it helps." He grinned. "Being a good shot might let you live a little longer, shoot a few more Mex."

Peaceful shook his head. "Squire, I must be an odd Tennessean. Sounds plum crazy. I seem to be the only man in the Alamo that don't want to kill a pile of Mexicans."

Squire Daymon blinked at Peaceful for a second. He sighed. "No, you ain't the only one in the Alamo that ain't exactly delighted at killin' Mexicans." He pointed across the patio. "Take Gregario Esparza. He's got kinfolks right over there, just across the river. And Jaun Abamillo. He lived in San Antonio all his life. And Juan Badillo. Fightin Mexicans is 'specially painful for them native-born Mexicans." He shook his head. "One o' these Mexicans in here fightin' with us has a brother out there. I know dyin' in here is gonna be more painful for him than it is for you and me. When you shoot a Mexican tomorrow, think of Gregario Esparza. He's in here fightin' his brother's out

147

there fightin' with General Santa Anna. Don't you know Gregario is going to wonder and worry when he aims at a Mexican soldier?"

Peaceful nodded. "Yes, I see what you mean. There's probably a lot of men in here that don't take kindly to killing." Peaceful took off one boot and poured the sand out on the ground. He laughed a sad fateful little quiet laugh. "You mentioned Gregario Esparza. He's got a brother out there. His little brother is a sergeant in General Santa Anna's army. I wonder what he will think when he goes to squeeze the trigger?"

"You go to sleep, boy. When you wake up, you'll feel better about it. When you wake up, you'll be fighting for your life."

"I don't need no sleep. I hope I'll be able to shoot, once somebody shoots at me. Besides, who wants to sleep?"

"Yeah." Squire Daymon turned on his side. "After tomorrow, you'll have eternity to sleep." Then he turned back to Peaceful. "How'd you get two hours' sleep?"

"Oh, I spent a while in the chapel, an' when I came out, I felt different. I felt calm and relaxed. I laid down and scratched some sand outta my hair and went right to sleep."

"Did'ja have a dream?" Squire Daymon asked.

"Yeah." Peaceful grinned. "How did you know?"

"Didn't know. I just always heard that when a man's close to death and can still go to sleep, well, sometimes he has an important dream. Sometimes a prophetic dream. Sometimes he dreams of what's to come."

"Mine was about my girl. Probably wasn't prophetic."

"Never can tell about dreams. What'd'ja dream, anyway?"

"Well, I dreamed I was back in Tennessee, on my horse Ole Blue, and my girl was ridin' behind me. We were on our way to Winchester, going to the courthouse to get married."

148

Johnny Hays raised his head up from its sleeping slope against the pallisade wall. "What'd'ja do?" he asked, suddenly wide awake at the mention of a woman. "Did ya get married?" Did ya get in bed with her? Git in her britches?"

"Oh shut up." Peaceful waved away Johnny's sudden interest. "I thought you were asleep."

"I was, but I woke up when I heard you say you was riddin' a horse with your girl on behind you. Don't you know better than to ride with your back to a girl?"

"Shut up," Peaceful laughed.

"Never turn your back to a girl. It's bad luck."

Peaceful waved away his words.

Johnny went on. "Did you marry her?"

"I don't know."

"What'd'ya mean you don't know? Tell us what you dreamed."

"I done told you. All I dreamed was that I was back in Tennessee and I was ridin' down Shaw Mountain with my girl hangin' on behind me."

"How was she holdin' you?" Johnny Hays leaned forward. "Did she have one arm around your chest and one around your neck?"

"Yeah, somethin' like that." Peaceful grinned. "She was holdin' me real tight like."

"Yeah, and you were headed to the courthouse to get married." Johnny leaned still further forward.

"That's all there was to it."

"You didn't even get to the courthouse?" Johnny asked, disappointed.

Peaceful shook his head.

"You didn't even get to the hotel with her?" His strained grinning face indicated he was really disappointed.

Peaceful shook his head.

"You didn't get in bed and get in her britches?"

Peaceful shook his head again.

"Damn, you can't even have a good dream!" Johnny Hays shook his head sadly.

Johnny was now shaking his head. "Happens ever'

time. Ever' time a man gets on a horse and puts a girl on back of him, ever' time he turns his back on a girl, he don't get in her britches."

Everybody laughed. Even Peaceful.

"A feller finds strange things in chicken houses." Johnny Hays was now wide awake, and he smiled that chicken eating grin of his. "Back there at the Summers place I was repairin' the hog pens while Peaceful and Squire was off roundin' up the hogs. And you know, ole Johnny Hays can work pr'tty fast if he wants to. I got them hog pens fixed pr'tty quick, and then I took a look at that chicken house." He grinned and blinked his eyes thoughtfully. "A feller finds some mighty strange things in chicken houses. In some chicken houses I have found wine, beer, and whiskey," he grinned sheepishly. "But when I opened that door to Mrs. Summer's chicken house, I wasn't expectin' to find nothin' in there but chickens. I had to look twice. I couldn't believe what I saw." He shook his head in remembrance. "This pr'tty little thing in white, she was tied to a cedar post with a leather thong. She was tied with just one hand, but she didn't seem to know how to untie it. She reached out to me with her free hand," Johnny stopped and looked around to be sure everybody heard that, "and she turned and tugged and tried to pull that thong loose from the cedar post." Johnny laughed a sly little grin. "Now old Johnny's tied up a woman or two-maybe they weren't fifteen-years-old fillies like this one-but this little gal, she couldn't even untie a leather thong that was just tied around one wrist. She reached out for me with her hand, and she still held her hand out toward me when I took out my knife to cut that thong. She rubbed her wrist for just a second. The she started moving toward me, unbottoning that white blouse and smiling at me. She reached out for me with both hands, and I began looking around that there chicken house for a bear trap. She had one hand on my shoulder when I led her out of that chicken house. By the time we got outside, she had her blouse off and was unbottoning my shirt. That gal reached for me.

150

She reached up there with them breasts and nuzzled them against my brown hairy chest. I was just fixin' to take her in my arms, and right then," Johnny Hays shook his head and heaved a loud sigh, "just as I reached for her, somebody started screamin'. It wasn't her screamin'. Her mama screamed and screamed." He shook his head again and used his finger to draw the outline of a woman's figure in the sand. He looked up. "Peaceful and Squire can tell you the rest. I got the top of my ear shot away just because I didn't turn her loose quick enough. Mrs. Summers told that Billy Summers to shoot off the top of my left ear, and before I even knew what she said, he done shot off the top of my right ear. A straight shot, that boy is. That rifle barrel of his rolls and wobbles around like a woman churning butter. I never did see him miss, though. I kept wonderin' where he would have hit if she had told him to shoot me between the eyes."

Everybody laughed, even Johnny Hays. Crockett leaned back and pounded his knees with his hands, howling and laughing so loud he could be heard down the Mexican lines.

32

Peaceful was sleeping fitfully, jerking and quivering, when he felt someone kick his boot. "Huh, what's that?" He jerked awake.

"Get up." A voice broke through the grey shadows of early daylight, and Peaceful made out the figure of David Crockett standing over him, gently kicking his foot. Crockett had his rifle cradled in his arm.

"What is it?" Peaceful rolled out of his blanket and grabbed his rifle.

"I hear men running out there." Crockett jerked his head toward his wood and cowhide wall.

A cannon blasted the dawn stillness. It came from the Mexican side of the river. Then a dozen cannons fired, and all the screams of hell descended on the Alamo. Cannons booming, drums beating their rolling thunder, bugles bleating, men screaming. The pallisade wall behind Peaceful shook.

The day was just being born when Peaceful ran with his rifle and climbed to the firing walk-way inside the wall. Peaceful ducked low as he ran along the wall to his post. He licked his thumb against his tongue and used his wet thumb to pull back the hammer on his rifle, resting the barrel against the top of the wall, and took aim. He wondered how much of this day would be his. Would he be alive when the sun rose and warmed the walls of the Alamo?

Dust and gunpowder burned Peaceful's eyes as he sighted down his gunbarrel. Through the mist of early dawn and dust and spent gunpowder, Peaceful made out a field of green and white and black. Like a meadow of wind-blown flowers. A running meadow.

A cannon fired from atop the chapel, and in the flash, Peaceful saw a wall of men in green and white with black tufted hats racing toward him, a wall of grim mustachioed Mexican troupers flashing their bayonetted rifles as they raced for the south wall of the Alamo. The attack was on!

A rifle roared to the right of Peaceful; another fired to his left. Peaceful stole a glance to his right at Squire Daymon, and then to his left at Little Joe Bayliss. They grinned as they blew on their barrels and pulled their ramrods to reload.

Peaceful looked back toward the south, at the line of charging soldiers. His rifle was loaded and cocked. He had to shoot. But which one? There were hundreds, all running and shouting and screaming.

Little Joe Bayliss's head jerked, his arms flew skyward, and he tumbled backward, off the firing platform. He hit the ground on his back. A leg kicked and his arm jerked. Then he lay still, with the left side of his face blown away, leaving only white bones and bloody flesh where his eyes had been.

Peaceful turned to his gun. "Well, they started it." He leaned his chin against his gun and shut one eye. He let the tip of his tongue stick out the corner of his mouth as he took a Tennessee aim. He pressed gently on the trigger and took a slow steady aim at a Mexican. Peaceful tightened his finger on the trigger. But he stopped and licked his dry lips. The Mexican was carrying a ladder! Not a gun! A ladder! Kill a man running with only a ladder in his hand? The Mexican was carrying it to lay against the wall so those behind him could climb the pallisade wall!

Crockett fired. Out of the side of his eye, Peaceful saw the belch of smoke from Crockett's gun and watched the man with the ladder crumble and fall. Crockett lowered his rifle with a grin. "Got four; how many you got?" He began reloading his stack of rifles.

"I ain't got any." Peaceful lowered his chin on the stock of his rifle. He beaded his sight on a green-sashed officer waving a saber as he ran toward the Alamo. Peaceful jerked as his rifle fired.

"That's better," Crockett shouted. "They'll never take our wall." He licked his thumb and lowered his rifle, jerking as the rifle kicked.

Peaceful stepped down from the firing platform to reload his rifle. He looked at his gun, staring at it unhappily. "I got one." He kept looking at his gun. Then he raised his head slowly to the dawn sky. "I killed! I killed a man!" He shook his head, thinking of his father back in Tennessee, slumped by a boundary tree, with a hole in his head. "I killed a man!" Peaceful stumbled as a splinter from a cannon shell ripped his left boot off his foot.

Crockett grabbed Peaceful by his coat and jerked his rifle out of his hand in a harsh quick jerk. He filled Peaceful's hand with one of Little Joe Bayliss's unfired rifles. "Damn right you killed a man. Now get up there an' get another one." He pushed Peaceful toward the firing platform.

Peaceful climbed the platform and took aim slowly. Behind him he heard Crockett laugh, "First one's allus a shock, ain't it boy?" Peaceful nodded as he aimed at the chest of a charging Mexican ten yards from the wall. Peaceful fired. Then he clung to his rifle, watching and pulled his ramrod. He began reloading his rifle. "The first 'un ain't 'zactly like shootin' a turkey, is it, Colonel?" Peaceful clenched his jaw and gave his head a little shake.

"Sho ain't." Crockett licked his thumb as he cocked his rifle and took aim slowly, then jerked gently as his rifle fired. He lowered his rifle, blew on the barrel, and began reloading. "Think I'd rather shoot turkeys," he grinned as he pulled a bullet out of his bullet pouch, gripped it with his teeth and dropped it out of his mouth into his rifle barrel. "Them turkeys don't shoot back."

Squire Daymon's rifle belched beside Peaceful, and Peaceful saw a green-sashed officer tumble back-

154

ward, grabbing his head as he fell.

Peaceful saw two dark hands reaching over the pallisade wall. He moved his rifle just as the black-hatted head of a Mexican soldier appeared at the top of the pallisade. Peaceful fired without aiming. The gun clicked, but didn't fire. It was empty! The Mexican blinked his eyes and continued climbing over the pallisade. Peaceful grabbed his rifle by the barrel and took two steps as he swung it at the Mexican striking him across the head of the ear, sending him sprawling in arm-swinging fury off the pallisade wall.

"Travis is shot!" Squire Daymon shouted, pointing toward the top of the north wall.

Peaceful turned in time to see Travis' shotgun tumble from his hands, still smoking from just having been fired, grabbing his head, stumbling down the cannon revetment in the center of the north wall. He fell to his butt at the bottom of the revetment. His body wobbled ungainly as Travis raised one hand to touch his bloody forehead. He brought his hand away and stared at the blood. He tried to raise to his feet, but wobbled so badly he fell. His slave, Joe, was at his side. Joe picked his master up in his arms and began carrying Colonel Travis toward Dr. Sutherland, who was running with his black bag, running toward the Commander of the Alamo.

Peaceful could see that Travis was dead, the way his arms hung down crazily as Joe walked slowly toward Dr. Sutherland.

Peaceful now had his gun loaded, but when he looked out over the pallisade, the Mexicans had turned away. They were running to the west, around the chapel. He fired and watched a Mexican drop, falling forward, clutching his ears, grabbing his head with both hands.

"They've breached the north wall!" Sergeant Ward shouted as he and Billy King tried to turn the eighteen-pounder to the north, to fire at the breach in the north wall.

"I said them damn Mexicans wouldn't come over my pallisade." Crockett leaned over, re-loading his rifle. "They came through Travis' north wall. God-damn him anyway," Crockett cursed as he raised his rifle and fired into the wall of Mexicans storming into the patio through the breached north wall.

The two four-pound cannons in the patio poured shot after shot into the breached north wall, but the Mexicans poured through the breach like a herd of stampeded cattle and raced for the cannons.

Peaceful found an un-fired rifle of Johnny Hays' and he got off a shot just as the Mexicans swarmed over the cannons and turned them around, firing at the fleeing Texans, who now ran into the horse stock-ade. Peaceful was loading his rifle when he saw Ole Blue struggling out of the horse stockade, limping to-ward Peaceful with his bloody left foreleg shot away. Ole Blue nickered and nodded his head before he fell inside the bloody patio with a leg-kicking last nicker.

Peaceful fired twice, his gun and Little Joe Bayliss' gun, as the Mexicans swarmed over the inner patio. He crouched low in the morning shadows of the Palli-sade wall, as he re-loaded. He moved fast as he watched the black-hatted Mexicans try to enter Jim Bowie's room near the northeast portal. Every Mexi-can that stepped into Bowie's doorway shuddered and tumbled backward. Then two rushed in, followed by three more. Peaceful heard the screams and shouts as he rammed home the ramrod and readied his rifle.

He looked about him. Squire Daymon, Little Joe Bayliss, and Johnny Hays were already dead. Peace-ful rose to his feet out of the shadows of the Pallisade wall. Only he and Crockett were still on their feet. Crockett fired his rifle and leaned forward through the powdered smoke, watching a charging Mexican fall. Crockett stepped backward and reached behind him for a loaded rifle, reaching his hand along the wall as he watched the charging Mexicans. There were no rifles leaning against the wall; they were all fired, on the ground, under trembling bloody bodies. Crockett grabbed a rifle by the barrel and swung it at a tall black-hatted Mexican charging with his bayon-et raised, flashing in the morning light. Crockett hit

156

```
Fic     Templeton, R. L.
TEM     Alamo soldier
```

		DATE DUE	